Thinking Life

Other books by Mark Anderson

Pure: Modernity, Philosophy, and the One
The Thinker-Artist (Sophia and Philosophia)
Plato and Nietzsche: Their Philosophical Art
Moby-Dick *as Philosophy: Plato-Melville-Nietzsche*
Zarathustra Stone: Friedrich Nietzsche in Sils-Maria

Thinking Life

A Philosophical Fiction

Mark Anderson

S.Ph.

S.Ph. Press
Nashville, TN

ISBN-13: 978-0-9967725-6-3
ISBN-10: 0-9967725-6-1

Library of Congress Control Number: 2017915357

www.sphpress.com

Table of Contents

Editor's Introduction   i

I. On the Decline of Our Educational Institutions   1

II. We Scholars   18

III. Divine Madness   43

IV. Hard Fate and Black Bile   60

V. The Wanderer and His Shadow   81

VI. The Art of Philosophy   116

Epilogue   139

Editor's Note   153

Alla famiglia Muccini

Editor's Introduction

In the body of a previous book (*The Thinker-Artist*) I included Professor Thomas Blair's narrative of the life and work of the late philosopher Michael Tommasi. At the core of Blair's account is a precis of a chapter of Dr. Henry Holet's scarce encyclopedic tome, *Obscure Thinkers Out of their Times* (1951), and the remainder derives from Blair's original research. Initially the professor intended this piece for the preface to his *Sophia and Philosophia*, a book which he eventually abandoned for reasons I recount in *The Thinker-Artist*. In any case, through my study of Thomas Blair I was attracted also to the enigmatic Michael Tommasi, and I have since continued Blair's research into Tommasi's intellectual biography. My initial efforts uncovered only a few stray scraps of new material, but recently I chanced upon a cache of documents which must be of momentous consequence for those few scholars engaged in Tommasi studies.

To make progress in this field is not easy. To make an authentic and significant discovery is nearly impossible. Tommasi was born January 3, 1889, in Torino, and he passed his youth in Italy through his graduation from the University of Urbino. He then moved with his parents to England, where he earned a Ph.D. in Philosophy from Cambridge in 1915. Later he passed a decade dwelling in monastic seclusion in Greece, specifically in Mystras, near Sparta. Later still he returned to England, and after a decade there spent mostly in isolation, he died in Cambridge in 1946. Tommasi's frequent relocations, and his predilection for solitude, make it difficult to track reliable details of his life and literary estate. Some of the works he is known to have produced are lost, either vanished altogether and forever, or secreted away in private collections. Other works mentioned in the literature may well amount to nothing more than rumors. And given Tommasi's hermetic habits, it is possible that writings by his hand exist which no one besides his closest friends or family ever heard of.

This brings me to my discovery. I should note to begin that my wife Francesca is Italian by birth. She hails from the Montefeltro region, province of Pesaro-Urbino, and like Tommasi she attended the University of Urbino (many years later, of course). Her family still resides in the small town of Mercatino Conca, an hour by car north of Urbino. We visit them every summer. Thus it happened that in June of 2016, while we were staying with her parents, my wife suggested we take an overnight trip to Urbino, which besides being the site of many fond memories of her early adulthood, is of interest also for having been an active center of intellectual life during the Renaissance, for there was the residence of the humanist duke, Federico III da Montefeltro, and the birthplace and childhood home of Raphael.

We made the trip to the hilltop town early on a Friday morning, navigating the winding roads in the family's Cinquecento. Then, after relaxing over cappuccinos and croissants in the bar of our hotel, we toured the university and the ducal palace. After a late lunch we visited an old bookstore—famed in fact as the oldest in the region—and while there we struck up a conversation with the proprietor of the place, an amiable old humanist whose family had founded the shop early in the nineteenth century. When in the course of our discussion I asked the man whether by chance he owned any works by or about Michael Tommasi, a look of excited surprise spread over his face. He rarely encountered anyone who knew that name, he said, and never before had a visiting American mentioned him. He himself knew little about Tommasi beyond the fact that he had once been famous in certain intellectual and artistic circles as an "eccentric philosopher-poet." He was however delighted by my own intimate knowledge of Tommasi's life, and at the conclusion of our talk he invited me and Francesca to dinner at his home later that evening.

Ludovico's apartment was located on the edge of the old town under the lee of the city wall, on the far end of a cramped section of labyrinthine lanes, but we located the place without much trouble by appealing to locals for assistance along the way. We arrived to find our host awaiting us on his terrazzo, and after an exchange of greetings he ushered us inside. His home was in the traditional style of pale brick, plaster, and rough wood beams, with the idiosyncratic touch that every room was elegantly cluttered with paintings, curios, papers, and books. Ludovico regaled us with stories about his various collections, which were so extensive an hour's tour hardly sufficed for a superficial survey. When later we sat down to eat we spoke of various subjects over the pasta, but with the second course we turned to discussing Michael Tommasi. We spoke of Tommasi's life and work through the rest of the meal, and we maintained the theme while lingering over coffee and drinks afterward. Ludovico was visibly fascinated by the information I shared with him, and he grew increasingly animated as the hours passed. Finally, near the end of the evening, after draining the last of his wine, he stood up and announced that he had recently acquired a collection from an old Urbino family which included material he believed would interest me. Then he left the room and descended into the basement. When he returned a few minutes later he carried a weathered old wooden crate marked in charcoal on one side with a single word, "Tommasi." I sat up in my seat, staring at Francesca, and when Ludovico placed the crate on the floor and removed the burlap covering, and I saw inside a hoard of madly disordered material, I could hardly believe my eyes. I had no idea what I was looking at, but I understood immediately that if there should be among the papers any work at all by Tommasi's own hand, this would be the find of my life.

To my surprise—indeed I was shocked—Ludovico offered to let me keep the material, asking only for my word to deal respectfully with any document of value I should happen to find. I was happy to give him my pledge, which I did while shaking his hand. Not long after this we left, and by taking turns with the load Francesca and I carried the crate back through town to our hotel. Immediately upon returning to her parents' home the following morning, I sorted through the contents of the crate sprawled out on the kitchen floor. Inside I discovered among numerous documents relating to Tommasi written by others, a large collection of material indisputably produced by the man himself. I believe in fact that several small leather-bound volumes, which were stacked in the bottom of the crate, are the journals on which Dr. Holet relied for much of his account of Tommasi's life, and which Prof. Blair complained of being unable to locate. I have not yet studied these closely, however, for I have concentrated my attention on a short manuscript, hand-written, revised throughout, and signed on the final page by Tommasi himself. It seems that neither Holet nor Blair knew anything about this work, nor is it mentioned specifically in any of the other relevant literature. But that it is authentically Tommasi's work cannot be doubted by anyone familiar with his handwriting.

Since the reader will soon encounter the work directly for himself (or herself, as the case may be), I say no more about it here than to summarize it as the intellectual-existential autobiography of Tommasi's imagined narrator, a university professor of philosophy, as recollected through the prism of his engagement with a "philosopher-artist" whom he befriends while on a convalescent summer sojourn in the Swiss alps.

But before turning the reader over to Tommasi himself, I should address a few editorial matters, beginning with the date of the manuscript's composition. Considering the substance and style of the work, Tommasi might well have written it not long after completing his doctoral thesis, for at that time he aimed to practice philosophy as (and here I cite Blair's precis of Holet's work, which includes quotations from Tommasi himself) "an 'experimental artistic endeavor' closely related to 'the forces of inspiration productive of poetry (of poetry as poetry or as novel),' as Dostoevsky had 'so masterfully conceived the novel as itself a mode of philosophy.'" That Tommasi has written on the first page of the manuscript, apparently by way of a subtitle, "A Philosophical Fiction," illustrates this conception of philosophy as an artistic endeavor intimately related to poetry.

Against an early dating of the piece is the narrator's position as a university professor, for it is at least questionable whether Tommasi would have imagined himself as such a character, having only just received his doctorate. Yet this objection is not decisive, for Tommasi's father was a professional academic, Tommasi himself was close with several of his Cambridge professors, and even in his earliest period he reflected on the philosopher's role in culture and the proper place of the love of wisdom in the philosopher's life, including his life as a scholar and academic. It is not therefore unthinkable that the manuscript is early after all.

Yet even if it is early, we should date it to a later phase of Tommasi's early period, say as close to 1919 or the spring of 1920 as possible, for references in the text to a recently concluded war suggest that Tommasi wrote with the aftermath of the First World War in mind.

The above considerations notwithstanding, the manuscript could well derive from Tommasi's middle period in Mystras, at which time he explored an experimentally Platonic way of thinking while yet infusing his ideas and prose with (to cite Blair again) "a Nietzschean mood." For although Tommasi suppressed the identity of the philosopher-artist befriended by his narrator, he evidently modeled the character on Nietzsche—though, to be sure, on a Nietzsche who is less an anti- or inverted-Platonist than one who, distinguishing Plato the individual from the tradition of Platonism, welcomes the influence of the creative thinker and writer while rejecting the dogmatic system. Thus there is a sense in which the work is infused throughout with a dual Platonic-Nietzschean spirit, a taut harmony fashioned from conceptual and existential oppositions and agreements.

Among the notes associated with the manuscript I have found no explanation for Tommasi's decision to mask his appropriation of Nietzsche's life and thought; but since the mask is semi-transparent, I assume he expected some of his readers to see through the disguise. Perhaps he hoped to liberate Nietzsche's philosophy from the bombast that was gathering around his name at the time, to set his ideas upright again on their original doves' feet. But I really cannot say for sure. In any case, if Tommasi did indeed compose this work during his time in Greece, we should date the text to the middle of the 1920s.

During Tommasi's final years in Cambridge, when he intentionally adopted "a non-academic style (of writing as well as of thinking)," his work was sufficiently experi-mental—from the perspective of traditional academic philosophy—that one can easily imagine him producing the manuscript during this period too. Professor Blair cites reports that at this time Tommasi was at work on a "vast poetic manuscript," which to this day has not been identified. It may be that he excerpted the work at issue here from this longer piece and later revised it to stand alone; it may also be that he composed the two independently but simultaneously. In either case we should probably date the manuscript to an early phase of this period, for there are no intimations in the text of a looming military conflict on the model of World War II.

The problem of dating is exacerbated by the fact that Tommasi seems intentionally to have obscured the internal chronology. The war to which the narrator refers is not obviously the First World War, yet social and cultural realities referenced in the text suggest a period between the two World Wars.

Uncannier still than this chronological eccentricity is the fact that the narrator's meetings and conversations with his friend in the mountains appear to take place in the nineteenth century (as of course they would have to do to involve Nietzsche), when on any rational, accurate account the narrator would either not yet have been born, or would have been but an infant. When in the mountains, it seems, the man is somehow out of time.

Nor is the temporal element the only problematic feature of the text. The action obviously takes place in Europe, but the specific location of the narrator's university is unclear, and his account of the institution has much in common with contemporary university life in America. This is not altogether a surprise, for Tommasi had an abiding concern with intellectual and cultural trends in the States, which he regarded as precursors to (even as primary causes of) events to come in Europe, and he maintained correspondence with peers in American universities. Surprising or not, this aspect of the text contributes to a dreamlike atmosphere which merges a concreteness of detail with a free-floating sort of historical displacement.

In sum, then, we may state with relative confidence that Tommasi produced the text sometime between 1919 and 1925-30. The narrative present seems to be set in the later part of this period, the immediate narrative past in the early 1920s, and the prior encounters with his friend in the mountains are set somehow as impossibly early as sometime in the 1880s.

I myself have formed no definite opinion as to when Tommasi composed the text, though I do suspect a date near the later end of the span noted in the previous paragraph. It may be that his journals or other documents included in the Urbino papers provide the solution to the riddle, but since I have not yet had the time to sort and scrutinize the relevant material, for now I leave the matter unresolved.

One last word about Tommasi's manuscript. It is written alternatingly in English and Italian, for although the narrator speaks and writes in English, his friend communicates exclusively in Italian. Tommasi himself was fluent in both languages from the days of his earliest childhood, his mother having been born and raised in London, his father in a small town in the southern Italian region of Puglia. Given these linguistic specificities, it is possible to read the manuscript as a narrative in which, and through which, Tommasi talks to himself about himself, or, more specifically, as a dialogue between different aspects of his philosophical personality. A spiritual autobiography, if you will, told by the author to himself for the purpose of self-exploration, expansion, descent and ascent.

That the biographical element of Tommasi's work may have for the reader an intellectual import beyond the mere satisfaction of a prying curiosity should not be doubted. It is true that many of those who document the lives of thinkers and artists are motivated by a perverse reductivist compulsion; they aim to track an idea or a style back to a source in some particular personal event, and thereby to "explain" the work by the life. The basest of such men aspire to demystify the work, to drain the art, and the artist, of any trace of apparent magic or genius. I myself am no such leveler or debunker. For me the value in studying the lives of thinkers and artists resides in the consequent insight into their manner of becoming who they were, insight one may incorporate into one's own life. Not by direct imitation, of course, for every man is an individual, and his habits of thought and action are particular, and particularly suitable, to himself alone. Yet one may well adapt for personal use the lessons learned from the lives of others. After all, the genuine student of philosophy aims for something more than scholarly knowledge of others' wisdom; he longs to attain to wisdom himself. Therefore I say he would do well to study the lives of admired philosophers, for in doing so he may learn what it takes to become a philosopher too. With this thought in mind, then, I suggest that the reader approach the biographical element of Tommasi's work as being of equal value with its more explicit intellectual and creative merits.

But to return to the linguistic eccentricities of Tommasi's manuscript: I have translated the Italian passages to render the work in English throughout, though I have retained the occasional Italian phrase to remind readers of the linguistic idiosyncrasies of Tommasi's original.

And while on this subject of language, I should note that Tommasi wrote the title, "Thinking Life," in English on the first page. I read a triple entendre in the expression, which would not come through in the corresponding Italian formulation. Therefore I assume that Tommasi intended the multiple ambiguities.

Finally, I have incorporated Tommasi's own revisions into the final manuscript, and whenever I have deemed it appropriate I have taken it upon myself to correct mistakes and revise for clarity. I have also standardized several eccentricities of spelling. Apart from these and other such editorial necessities, however, I have made every effort to keep myself out of the work altogether. Michael Tommasi was more than capable of speaking for himself, and although he addressed the public only infrequently, his words were always well chosen, his ideas as stimulating as imaginative. It is my pleasure, and my honor, to provide him the platform to communicate once again. Therefore I now offer you the heretofore unavailable work,

Thinking Life: A Philosophical Fiction
by Michael Tommasi

I

On the Decline of Our Educational Institutions

I returned to the high mountain valley many years after my initial acquaintance with the man, who had later become a friend, though an age had passed since last we'd been in company together. Correspondence sustained me during the periods of our separation, but as a variety of intellectual, psychological, and spiritual frustrations had lately produced a pressure in me expanding almost to the point of bursting, I needed to see him again, if only to walk in the rejuvenating air of his presence. Thus it was I went into the mountains. To find him. It was for this I had gone the first time too, though of course I hadn't known this then.

The summer of our first meeting I was a professor free for the season, officially at liberty but practically often at my desk, reading and writing, erecting buttressed edifices of research and argumentation; also in the afternoons taking the cure at a local sanatorium. He was the carefree philosopher-artist travelling abroad, or rather idly wandering, creatively replenishing the storehouse of his intellect and imagination…

Or was I the free-spirited thinker and he the diligent scholar? These days it's a labor to recall, though less from the fading of memories than from finally overcoming such distinctions, the interblending of types, effected over the course of many intervening years.

But I should begin my story from the beginning.

Last year, after a decade teaching philosophy at a respectable (if not prestigious) provincial university, I had finally had enough of my "work-life," as the technocrats are pleased to call it. I was indifferent and uninspired. Hostile even. Ten years suffices for any routine, I say; and one should change one's life at least once every decade. Certainly one should change one's job. Jobs kill, sometimes by undermining the health of one's body, always eventually by crushing one's spirit. Which is not to denigrate work or activity, mind you. To the contrary. Activity is noble, natural, the actualization of one's proper potential. Jobs on the other hand exploit the innate tendencies of human nature, and the biological facts of human need, and divert them toward adventitious ends, specifically the ends of consumption or the accumulation of capital. Social and corporate propaganda induce the masses to spend money which often isn't theirs (which rather belongs to their creditors) to satisfy desires manufactured toward the end of increasing the wealth of the few. And more often than not these few—these Associates of the Board, these Executive Administrators, these Presidents of the institution—are a herd of lowing philistines.

Oh, when the seeking of wisdom is debased into a petty job-seeking!

It is fitting that the origins of the word "job" are unknown, cloaked in the shadows of shame, hidden under a rock. Appropriate too is the speculation that the word derives as a variant of the word *gobbe*, meaning a "mass" or "lump," as in a masticated glob of matter rolling around inside one's mouth. A suitably distasteful image, that.

Johnson defined "job" thus: "A low mean lucrative busy affair. Petty, piddling work." As a verb the word has meant, from as long ago as early in the eighteenth century, "to pervert public service to private advantage." From such lowly origins has the job ascended the summit of our most eager desire! This is the world we've built for ourselves, the environment to which we've adapted, the lives we've rashly chosen to live: with every passing year, with every annual expansion of the grasping reign of the "business man," abetted by ever more subtle refinements of mass-marketing and advertising schemes, formerly independent adults are pressured to join the "work force," or deceived into believing that as paid laborers they will discover their liberation. Freedom through work and wages! In reality these workers are servants dragged beneath the wheel of a degrading system, slaves of the basest sort of master, the corporate functionary, the Manager. And "job," according to Johnson, may also mean "a sudden stab with a sharp instrument."

Having said all this, I admit that no one observing the conditions of my own employment would regard me as a wage-slave. I live and work among the so-called "intellectual classes," who enjoy a degree of leisure unavailable to those whose labor consists primarily of bodily toil. I earn my living (a brutal expression!) with my mind, tongue, and pen, which is to say that I am paid to think, talk, and write. I am, in short, a university professor, endowed with all the rights and privileges pertaining to the position. For example, my employers formally encourage my intellectual and expressive freedom. Not that they appreciate, or even understand, this sort of freedom. But they superintend an operation whose lifeblood is uninhibited theoretical exploration; and although they would gleefully eliminate every manifestation of culture beyond their boorish comprehension, they would never actually apply such pressure as to finally still the heart of the beast that funds their salaries.

Before the war one could expect a certain nobility even among the masters of industry. They were generally men of good breeding, well-reared and properly educated, so even those members of their caste unmoved by a genuine love of art and ideas at least bore a grudging respect for those who cherish the finer things, deferred at least in certain spheres to the curators of the higher realms of the heart and mind. So degrading was the late conflict, however, so barbarously dehumanizing, that noble ideals were stacked and buried in the trenches with the best of our youth. Years on, and still they have not been excavated.

And, oh, the barrage of disinformation and deceit launched against the citizenry by their own governments! The crude expressions of chauvinism, hysteria, contrived outrage and sentimentality pushed by the party hacks and ideologues in the blotted pages of their newspapers, magazines, and nasty political pamphlets! So routine were these practices during the long years of war, so effective were they in influencing public opinion, even in shaping— or rather distorting—our ideas of human value, that they linger in our discourse, public as well as private. By now they inform our very self-conceptions. Today we voluntarily do the bidding of those who would degrade us. In short, quite apart from sacrificing countless lives to no good purpose, the last great war stomped with its bespattered boots heavy on the neck of human culture.

Post-war technological innovations—always only for the good, according to our cultural Brahmins—have in reality precipitated our decline. Military developments, to the production of which the bulk of our financial and scientific-intellectual resources were directed during those awful years, were afterwards adapted to non-martial ends. Our traditional social order was thereby fundamentally trans-formed, and the revolution was packaged and sold to us as an assortment of conveniences, labor- and time-saving devices, facilitators of our ease. Yet this technologized industrial world turns out to be more hectic and chaotic than ever. Anxiety and dis-ease increase. The fact that certain forms of pleasure and diversion are more accessible to greater numbers of people does not alter this; it only distracts us from the inevitable consequences. We no longer have time for the free play of the spirit. There is time only for work and "fun." The vapid and the vacuous. Worse, so surrounded are we by our novel devices that we have come to believe only in the now, the new and artificial. We have lost contact with the old, to say nothing of the eternal. These days are we not almost entirely separated from the world of nature?

Since the conclusion of the war the city has become our All. The mechanized urban world of material goods and bodily pleasure has migrated to the center of our consciousness, has become the focus of our attention and desire. These changes, moreover, have expanded and solidified the monetization of our lives, transforming our species by the quarter into a *homo economicus*. I have complained that recent revolutionary transformations were "packaged and sold" to us, and this is more than a figure of speech. The corporations that design and develop new technologies give no thought to promoting or supporting our moral or existential improvement; they operate exclusively for their own enrichment. In recent years they have even begun to manufacture modified versions of their products to sell to children, not because children need or naturally desire them; but the young are easily manipulated into craving them, and once accustomed to owning and using them, once dependent on them, they can be counted on to purchase the authentic so-called "mature" versions of these products when they enter the marketplace themselves by securing their own jobs.

I am reminded of an experience from not long after the war. A friend and I were walking through the woods, relaxing, conversing, occasionally stumbling on a hastily covered cache of expended shell casings. As our talk turned to the degradation of intellectual, cultural, and even of spiritual life effected during the war, we grew agitated and raised our voices, despairing at the futility of working toward a renaissance. Of course we would strive to maintain our personal aspirations, but there seemed no hope for the rehabilitation of public institutions supportive of a life as any other than an economic affair. The machine of industry was designed to be ever-expanding, and its gears and belts swept everything up into its blind grinding mechanism. We bewailed the ugliness of it all, barking complaints in bursts of rage, so furious our bodies shook, our blood afrenzy, and we flailed as if to strike at invisible powers. Finally, to exorcize our violent energy, we broke into a run. We raced through stands of pine, leapt over stones, crashed through thickets of brush and were scratched by thorny branches. Our arms and cheeks bled.

Then suddenly we saw two deer standing quiet across the way. A doe feeding with her fawn at the base of an old stone-pine. We stopped and stood in place, our arms relaxed by our sides. We fell silent, our breathing slowed.

The deer seemed not to notice us, though the mother looked up to survey her surroundings whenever the little one knelt down to graze. Occasionally the fawn nuzzled the doe's flank and she turned her head to snuffle at its neck. A thin mist played around their hooves and knobby ankles.

As we watched the deer we ourselves eventually decompressed, unmoored from our mundane concerns and eased into the environment around us. We became one with the trees, the rippling leaves, and the angled shafts of sunlight. We became one with the underbrush, one with the soil, one with the buzzing insects and twittering birds. We sank somehow into a primordial realm of the spirit, blurred and merged into the unity of nature, indistinct and indistinguishable. Nothing existed but a universal silent stillness. The mild cosmic hum.

Then the crackling snap! of a tree trunk or broken branch disturbed the deer. They started, hurried off, and disappeared.

The spell was broken. The world rushed back in a pandemonium of sights and sounds, and we too were ejected from the whole, stood out once again as isolated individuals over against the world, separated one from the other, divided even within ourselves. The restless return of multiplicity. Overwhelmed by the experience, my friend and I exchanged mystified glances, then turned around and headed back to town. On our way through the woods we kept silent, for all the world as if we feared the lives to which we were then returning.

I can't say what my friend was thinking on our way home, but I myself was lost in meditative reveries on the relative value of nature and art. I thought: I, who have been moved to tears by more than one of Michelangelo's masterpieces, have stood at times before these same works altogether unmoved. I have for example sat on the marble step in the church of San Pietro in Vincoli observing Michelangelo's *Moses* and discerned no beauty in the thing but only technical proficiency. The figure's muscled left arm is a marvel of realism, to be sure; his beard an impressive evocation in the medium of immobile stone of curls flowing almost like water; and compared to the sculptures by other hands surrounding it, the *Moses* is undeniably an astounding achievement. But must it always take my breath away? Must it always strike me as beautiful? For the truth is that it doesn't. At times one can feel even somehow ridiculous, gawking as if the work were a mystic marvel because, for example, the limbs are so very lifelike. Why shouldn't they be? They were carved by a master craftsman with the intention to render them so.

Ah, one has seen it all so many times. One is bored. One sighs and moves on.

Yet I have experienced no such tedium when contemplating nature's works. Even a simple pastoral scene, say of rolling hills, a patchwork of variously colored fields, bordered by narrow stands of cypress and pine, as one sees for example throughout central Italy—even such views of modest nature have about them an endless fascination and inexhaustible beauty.

Perhaps this is the truth in Plato's account of the relative value of artifacts, natural objects, and metaphysical essences. For whether or not we accept his theory of Forms, or his ontological and epistemological hierarchies, we may certainly agree that nature is somehow more beautiful, and at least in this sense more valuable and more real, than even the greatest of man's artistic accomplishments. In short, even a humble pair of deer, and the common trees and flowers in the forest surrounding them, are superior—even infinitely superior—to the inventions of Michelangelo's overwhelming genius.

Of course I had come to similar insights prior to this encounter with the deer, and I have had them since as well. This particular episode is memorable for the pronounced contrast between my specific mental states before the encounter and after, but overall it was not unique in its general features. And this provokes a question pertinent to my story: why is it that most every healthy human descends into a contemplative mood immediately upon observing a deer in the woods? It is true that this does happen, is it not? Imagine a man afoot in a woodland, agitated; imagine him unburdening himself of a garrulous gushing of words; imagine him in a sporting spirit or a violent passion; imagine him in love. Now picture to yourself this same man catching sight of a deer. Do not all haste and anxiety immediately flee from him? Does not his heart beat less rapidly? Does he not stand still as if in a dream or a meditative swoon? Yes, I am sure that he does.

Now ask yourself why this should be so. I say it is the stark encounter with nature. Something in our spirit knows that finally we have come home to the universal mother, merged with the innocent flow of becoming, that dark realm from which the thieving titan snatched us through the flame of self-reflective awareness. These I think are the deeper strata of the experience. But the effects of even the shallower layers are remarkable too. Every direct encounter with nature liberates us from the fabricated world in whose angular steel we daily enact our artificial roles. Street-sweeper, secretary, bond-trader, retailer; cabman and engineer; actuary and C.E.O; actor and academic. We did not evolve to inhale rubbish or to ingest iron filings, to slink about in the chill shadows of city skyscrapers, rarely beholding the sun or stars, to serve like drones the monotonous rounds of the factory conveyor belt, to "punch the clock." The deer reminds us of our proper place in the natural order.

It is true that since we children of nature are the progenitors of mechanism and industry, the urban landscape of our construction is itself in a way a natural thing. Yet its fundamental unnaturalness is no less a fact. Natural life unobstructed begets natural life, as we do ourselves through the biological act of procreation. Nature as *physis* as internal principle of motion and change. But our feats of mechanical engineering produce only sterile artifacts, dead things to which, madly, we sacrifice our living selves. An author of my acquaintance has written that in nature we encounter the mind of God and thereby are uplifted, whereas artifacts externalize the will of man, through which we are debased. There is a worthy insight here, or so it seems to me, even if I cannot assent to every assumption or implication of the thought precisely as expressed. The city is a source of alienation, both as a slab of synthetic matter dividing us from the skin of the earth, also as the locus of factitious routines that sever us from the purity of our innate human needs and inclinations. And one day even the green stretches between our cities will be cleared and overrun—the whole great round globe a uniform urban mass of clamor and commotion, a hurly-burly unending and unrelieved. This, with no haven of wood or deer for retreat.

Oh, life in this modern world is so ignoble, mean, and ridiculous that one can't even call it tragic. Yet neither is it comic, for no one is laughing from high-spirited merriment.

Such melancholy thoughts as these were worrying me as I sat before the window of my office on the morning on which my story properly begins. Powdery flakes of snow were falling to ground on the lawn, blanketing the earth in layers of repose. The dirty grey buildings of the city in the distance were obscured, the drone of its waking bustle muted, and all the world seemed pure, asleep and lost in innocent dreams. Troubled as I was by somber reflections, I was yet also at my ease. For sometimes it is comforting to nestle in one's wistfulness, a posture that radiates an emotional warmth, as when in winter one wears a sweater indoors or lounges before the hearth fire.

But my morning's reverie was not to last. A sharp knock disturbed my meditative quietude, and an envelope appeared beneath my door. A beige thing stamped with the crisp shameless lettering of bureaucratic officialdom. Inside was a memo issued by the so called "Senior Administration" of my university. A fresh directive of chores to add to those announced earlier in the year.

"Every full-time employee shall henceforth, in addition to his or her regularly contracted obligations, discharge specific clerical duties as determined by Senior Administration and delegated by area Supervisors, including but not limited to etc. etc...

"Employees shall accomplish allocated tasks no later than the date as indicated by the relevant Supervisor upon issuance of notification, this date to be determined by the Supervisor, but never to exceed two weeks, or ten full working days, following the official allocation of assignments. Appeals and requests for accommodation shall be presented, in writing on official institutional letterhead, no later than twenty-four hours after receipt of designated assignments, to the employee's immediate Supervisor, it being solely his responsibility to determine which appeals, if any, merit the attention of Senior Administration. In such cases final adjudication resides with Senior Administration in consultation with the Board.

"We need not remind the staff that regular refusal to comply with the above directive shall result in official reprimands, with notices recorded on permanent file. Especially egregious violations may be punishable by termination on grounds of insubordination, subject to official review by Senior Administration and the Board.

"In closing let us stress how very much we value your contribution to the spirit of this great university. We thank you in advance for your participation in our many exciting new endeavors. Etc. etc…"

The imposition of trifling new responsibilities extraneous to my regular obligations was now almost a monthly routine. And of course there was no negotiating. The much heralded "shared governance" ostensibly operative within the institution was no reality but only empty verbiage, claptrap disseminated for public consumption. One simply had to bite one's fist and submit. For example, the University Council's unanimously affirmed objection to the recent demand that professors increase the number of students in their lectures and tutorials, and that they document their activities by the hour on printed "schedule matrices," all in the name of "efficiency, on the model of the most profitable corporations in our region"—this official protest was issued to no effect whatever.

Complying with these persistent demands to execute trivial clerkish chores beyond the bounds of my academic expertise, and to conduct myself as an employee of a commercial firm tasked only with maximizing profit—this sapped the enthusiasm I'd formerly felt for my life as a thinker, writer, and teacher, a life on all counts more to be cherished than the tedium-death of administrative drudgery.

Thus I grew more restive with every additional dictate, and the futility of reasoning with my superiors enflamed my frustration and resentment.

Over the course of several days following my receipt of this latest notification I brooded on my discontent until it hatched into a fit of rage. Late one afternoon before departing for the day I typed a memo of my own, addressed it to the Senior Administration, and deposited it in the mail bin on the reception desk of my departmental suite.

Dear Sirs,

I write to you today to offer my assistance, for it strikes me that you formulated your recently propagated expectations of staff and faculty while suffering from an especially virulent strain of cognitive blight. My fear is that you have lost your wits, and that consequently you have misapprehended the relevant state of affairs. That is to say, you seem to believe that we professors have too little work to do. If this is so, I should like hereby to relieve you of the fancy that has lately bewitched your faculties. I can only assume that the proximate cause of your condition is ignorance of the nature of intellectual life, itself resulting from your living always under the influence of the grubby lust for money. I am sure that men who occupy your station, and who staff such managerial positions as yours, cannot easily help themselves. You are business men after all, and it is your business to increase revenue.

I know that some of you are fond of boasting of having once practiced as pedagogues yourselves; but I also know—as does every other instructor associated with this institution—that no genuine educator desires to inhabit the bland domain of administrative bureaucracy. *Not for any stretch of time. Oh, yes, one or another academic might be tempted occasionally; this is only natural, and due to our own brand of ignorance. But immediately the conditions and consequences of such a life are revealed, every true thinking man will throw up his hands and hurry back to his books and students.*

Books and students—it seems that I must stress to you the following point, namely, that a professor's vocation is to read and speak of books with his students. Also to conduct research, to think, and perhaps from time to time to conceive and compose his own written works. This appears to you a frivolous waste of time, I am sure. You imagine that we are malingering when we might instead be busy identifying and exploiting fresh 'revenue streams,' as I believe you refer to those whom men of my cast of mind call, simply, 'people.'

Is it possible that you overlook the fact that your river of lucre will evaporate if you neglect to infuse it with the elements necessary to its flourishing? Must you be reminded—even if you think so meanly of yourselves as to conceive your function as university officials to act as hawkers of goods and services—must you really be reminded that if you are to act as salesmen you must have access to a store of the relevant items on offer? And of the highest quality? Surely you understand that no business can flourish on the memory of former glory, especially if the report is spread abroad that the place no longer merits its reputation. To put the matter frankly in terms you will appreciate: there will be no demand if you have nothing to supply. Now, the demand at issue is an education. But as you are not yourselves competent to meet this demand, you have need of scholars and teachers to supply it on your behalf, and they in turn require from you the provision of the resources to do their work well, unencumbered by needless burdens.

Therefore I conclude by suggesting that you see to the mundane business of fattening your bankbooks, and allow us scholar-educators to keep our heads and hands pure of crass concerns, that we might be at liberty to do what we know best how to do, which is to learn, and to share our learning with interested students.

In other words and in short, in future please resist the urge to augment our responsibilities with the numerous little inane tasks that properly belong to you and your administrative staff.

Sincerely, etc.

I suppose it goes without saying that the recipients of my analyses and advice were none too happy with my input. Or, rather, with me, personally. They communicated their displeasure to my area Supervisor, presumably quite vigorously, and he in turn called a meeting at which he informed the gathered members of several departments that the recent directive of Senior Administration was really quite unremarkable, that staff at similar institutions labored contentedly under comparable expectations, and he implied moreover that recalcitrant personnel were malcontents ungrateful for the opportunities our employment provided us. Had there been any doubt anteriorly, he thereby proved himself a flunky enforcer of his superiors' every whim, no matter how ill-considered, rather than an aid and ally of those for whose benefit he was supposed to advocate.

The following day I was summoned to meet with representatives of the Senior Administration. I dreaded the event, but more than that the whole affair infuriated me. To be subject to the power—I do not say authority—of such crass bureaucrats, who knew little, and cared even less, about the true substance and mission of the institution they managed, was deeply dispiriting. The rage came from the hopelessness of change.

But I defer any further treatment of these matters until I have introduced a theme more immediately relevant to the substance of my story. My first trip into the mountains.

II

We Scholars

As a graduate student in my late twenties, I began one winter to experience attacks of migraine fever while conducting research for my doctoral thesis. Long hours sitting alone in the basement rooms of university libraries, hunched over a creaking desk, chasing down references to obscure manuscripts, translating ancient languages from small-print editions of old books, copying extended extracts into my notes, formulating and recording my own insights and arguments—all this intellectual labor executed while hidden away from the sun drained me of the vigor I'd acquired as a child on walking tours with my father. I lost weight; I grew sallow and weak; my eyesight deteriorated and the pains in my head, ranging from mild but persistent annoyances to incapacitating afflictions, befell me at least once a month. During the worst periods I suffered every fortnight. Sometimes I could not leave bed for whole days through. Yet despite these nagging aggravations I persevered, and my thesis was very well received. Just six months after I took my degree I assumed the professorial chair that I occupy even to this day.

My first three years in the position were extraordinarily productive, despite the persistence of many physical infirmities. Publication followed publication, and my reputation as a meticulous scholar amplified with each new work. I was invited to lecture at neighboring universities, and students enrolled in my department to study with me and my colleagues. My own work centered on comparative analyses of argument forms in the Platonic dialogues, but in our department we specialized in every branch of ancient philosophy, particularly as practiced by the Greeks. Through our efforts, with the invaluable assistance of colleagues in the department of philology, a steady issue of keen young Hellenists flowed out to enrich the cultural life of university towns throughout the region. Would that their influence had persisted through the barbaric years of war! But I have said as much as I intend to say for now regarding the state of contemporary culture. Here I mean to discuss my personal situation, particularly as pertains to my intellectual-spiritual condition.

During the early years of my professorship, my health improved incrementally. Thoroughly disabling spells of pain were rare. Yet my headaches did not cease altogether, and they often interfered with my work. Moreover—whether as a consequence of my pain, or originating in a more fundamental source, I could not then say—I was subject to dreary melancholic moods. These facts were evident to my colleagues, who worried for my health, and my closest friend among them regularly encouraged me to take a cure at a celebrated sanatorium in the mountains of southern Switzerland. Eventually I relented and heeded his advice.

Thus it was that eight years ago this month, on the morning of the summer solstice, I boarded a train bound south for Locarno by way of the St. Gotthard Pass and a transfer at Bellinzona. That night I slept in a rustic old hotel beside the shore of Lake Maggiore, and early the following morning I lumbered up the steep switchback road into the mountains in a wobbly post-chaise carriage, an anachronistic mode of transportation which evoked in me the dreamlike impression of travelling back into the heart of the previous century.

I quote the following observations from the notebook I kept that summer:

Maggiore is vast, seems endless. To the north, high forested mountains with exposed granite walls slope down to the water. Villages and isolated farms along the shore. Lazy herds of grazing cattle. Bleating sheep. Architecture reminds me of my youth, somehow rather of my father's youth. Mercury-silver water. Wind. Whitecap waves. (Water dark green when calm.) Small fishing boats. ... Oh, I nodded off into semi-consciousness, a hypnogogic state. Heavy head. How long was I out? ... Here apparently a resort town. Yellow and cream colored houses, clay-tile roofs, built into the slopes. Hotels. ... Taller snow-capped mountains now, the high Alps looming. Into the massive foothills, the incline gradually increasing. ... The road now twisting up beside a ravine cut by a broad stream, or rather a cascade, translucent green water, sun bleached rocks, white water splashing, at intervals infused with narrow run-off falls from the surrounding peaks. ... My head bobs with the rocking carriage. Meditative state, a sort of waking dream. ... Here a small plateau, a quiet hamlet, the central descending falls dammed up to form a lake. Distinctive alpine flowers now and architecture too (wood-framed windows, elegant designs carved into the plaster quoins). Beyond this the incline steepens and the turns sharpen. Colder now. Pressure in the head. My ears explode. High peaks in the distance before us appear quite near. Goats. Hollow bells. Approaching our destination now, steeper still, hairpin turns.

… At last! Level ground and open skies. The Val di Sogno! Spreading meadows carpeted with shining yellow flowers. High mountain peaks massed along either side of the valley, running north. Lakes between reflecting the scene.

Upon entering the little village at the near end of the valley, five-thousand feet above the sea, I rented a room in a small hotel nearby the sanatorium grounds. I was reluctant to reside in the spa's available rooms, for as I was unfamiliar with the regimen and routine of such a place, and therefore somewhat wary of it, I had no desire to commit myself entirely to its discipline. I secured reservations for the afternoon sessions of gymnastic training and hot-spring bath immersions, these activities followed by a modest meal of greens prescribed by the staff nutritionist. I intended to participate completely if I experienced notable improvements, but in the meantime I reserved my mornings and evenings for time alone in study and relaxation.

I had arranged to arrive a few days prior to the beginning of my sessions, my intention being to take the time to explore my new surroundings at my leisure. Therefore after signing for my room and resting an hour with a cold compress on my eyes, I unpacked my luggage and stepped outside for a walk. The experience was stimulating, simultaneously calming and invigorating. The expansive meadows blooming in a profusion of color; lakes lapping serene against tufted shores; towering chains of mountains forested green, granite scored, and peaked with snow; the sky a rounded canopy of an infinitely translucent blue—an hour's perambulation in the thin delicious air was as a passage through a master's living portrait of nature sublime. That afternoon I did not doubt that the sun really is an offspring of the Good.

I returned to my room in the early evening psychically refreshed but weary, also with a throbbing behind my eyes. The activities of the day, as delightful as they had been, drained me. Therefore after eating a thick slice of bread with wine, I sat some time in the dark to rest my eyes, then went to bed. Thankfully I had no trouble falling to sleep, and for ten straight hours I floated in a dreamless state of unconsciousness. I awoke the next morning slowly, but feeling thoroughly revitalized. I was excited by the prospect of a day unburdened by the nuisances of travel and with long stretches of free time to occupy according to the velleities of my mood.

My first thought on rising from bed was of the research in which I was then engaged. Therefore, since I had carried my papers and several volumes of relevant scholarship in my luggage, I sat down to study before breakfast. After less than an hour of close reading, however, an acute pressure behind the skin butted against the backside of my forehead, causing my vision to waver and blur. The experience was not unfamiliar. Immediately I laid the book aside and closed my eyes, and I sat very still in this posture for several minutes, breathing with intention. This therapeutic was generally efficacious if initiated promptly on the first surge of discomfort, as on this occasion I had managed to do. Hence the pain subsided, at which point I dressed and went downstairs to eat.

A Philosophical Fiction

After breakfast, in accord with the maxim that he who takes one hundred steps after a meal will live for ninety-nine years, I left the hotel for a walk outside. I intended to explore the grounds of the sanatorium, which were vast and handsomely manicured, but on the way I was distracted by a man proceeding in the opposite direction. He nodded politely as he passed, a mischievous gleam in his eye, and he rolled lightly in his stride with a gay sort of musicality. Yet there also moved about the man a spirit of seriousness, as if his brightness emanated from a core of molten steel. Most striking of all was the book he carried under his arm, for although my view was obstructed, I was sure the spine was impressed with the words, "PLATONIS DIALOGI." The Dialogues of Plato.

I turned around to watch the man as he walked away, intermittently eyeing his book and scrutinizing his singular comportment. His head sat ponderously on his shoulders, its weight accentuated by his manner of hanging it over his chest as he walked. Yet his feet moved almost like a dancer's, his step expressive of cheerfulness. I watched him until he disappeared behind an outcrop of fir trees beyond which the path wound through a meadow toward a nearby lake. Twice he stopped to study his book, and on each occasion, after closing the volume and tucking it under his arm, he withdrew a little notebook from his jacket pocket, stood for a moment in concentrated thought, then jotted down his musings and moved on. Eventually, as I say, I lost sight of him behind the copse of fir.

Later that evening in my room I thought much of the man. The spirit of his surprising demeanor enchanted me—

the harmonization of apparent opposites, the reconciliation of shadow and light, resembling less a twilit dusk than breaking dawn. In brief, the partnered notes of depth and joy. Of course all this might well have been a fantasy of my own projection. I knew nothing of the man after all, had seen him only once and for only a few minutes at that. But there was also the intrigue of the book. Reckoning all the relevant facts, I could not dismiss the thought that here was a mystery I must pursue, and that moreover in its resolution lay something like my own salvation.

The following morning, after another attempt to study foiled by pain, I left the hotel and encountered the man once again. Again we were headed in opposite directions, I toward the sanatorium grounds, he toward the lake. And again he greeted me with an air commingled of gravity and joviality, then passed on, stopping from time to time to read his book and take his notes. On this day, however, when he paused on the path just prior to passing behind the outcrop of trees near the lake, as he removed his notebook from his pocket another item slipped out and fell to the ground. Apparently the accident escaped his notice, for he soon walked on without retrieving his property. Overcome by curiosity, and taking the event for an opportunity to introduce myself, I hurried down the path toward the abandoned article on the ground—a folded piece of paper, quite obviously covered front and back with penciled printing. Resisting the urge to read it, I slipped the paper into my pocket and continued along the path in pursuit of the man.

He was now not too far ahead of me, for he had stopped to sit on a bench in the meadow beside the path. He was neither reading nor writing but staring straight ahead, contemplating—or so it seemed to me—the sublime scenery before him, the multicolored streaming bands of wildflowers, the mountains rising in magnificent piles of green, grey, and white, their frozen summits shimmering against a bright blue sky, and all this beauty enjoying too a mirror-existence reflected in the crystalline waters of the lake. I did not want to startle the man, so I approached to the side of his bench and waited for him to notice me. When he did, I smiled and said, "Excuse me, sir. I don't mean to disturb you, but I believe you dropped this back there on the path," and as with one hand I gestured toward the trees, with the other I removed the folded paper from my pocket and held it out to him.

"*Oh, sì, credo che tu abbia ragione*," he said, reaching out to take the paper from my hand. And after inspecting it he stood up and shook my hand, a broad smile expanding beneath his thick moustache. "Yes, yes!" he beamed. "Quite right! And my thanks to you for it, sir. *Grazie! Grazie infinite!* You have done me a most thoughtful kindness, most kind indeed, so hard-won are the thoughts I've recorded here, so vital to my well-being, past and future alike. And in the present moment, too, naturally."

My first impression of the man was of one possessed of an amiable spirit, generous with an evident store of goodwill. Yet his manner was charged with an undercurrent of severity, as if he deliberately held some part of his soul in check. The result of this tension was electric, magnetic even, and I confirmed then my earlier suspicion that this was a man I very much wanted to know.

As we stood exchanging introductions, I stole a glance over his shoulder at the book on the bench behind him. PLATONIS DIALOGI: Vol. I. So I was right! But then who was this man before me? Who was this stranger reading Plato in the Greek while ambling among the wildflowers? I knew, or knew of, most all the scholars of ancient philosophy worth knowing in Europe. But I had never before seen this man, nor ever encountered his name.

Reasoning that no lover of Plato would scruple to share his passion with a fellow admirer, I inquired of him directly, "How comes it, sir," I asked, indicating the book on the bench, "how comes it that you are walking through this striking landscape with a volume of Plato under your arm? That is—if you don't mind my asking—are you by chance a student of the Greeks?"

"Ah, yes, well, but aren't we all?" he replied, and the gleam I'd noted the previous morning shone once again in his eye. "That is to say, is not every one of us educated Europeans a student of the Greeks, for better or worse?" And speaking thus he retrieved his book and with a gesture suggested we walk as we conversed. I followed his lead and walked beside him toward the lake.

"But, to be quite serious," he resumed, "I was once something of a professional student of the Greeks. For every teacher is a student, is he not? Every earnest teacher, to be sure."

He then proceeded to explain that he had once been employed as a professor at university, but he was vague as to the details. He seemed to have retired, though he was not at all the age for it. From what I could make of his account, I inferred his discipline must have been either philosophy or philology, and this prompted me to speak of my own work, to which he responded with, "Ah, a *Chiarissimo Professore*! I see. But then what are you doing away from your desk? That is to say, if I may put your question back to you, what are *you* doing under this radiant sky *without* a volume of scholarship under your arm?"

We laughed together at his remark then turned onto the path that wound around the lake. Later, when the way sloped into a forested stretch on a rise above the shoreline, I directed our conversation to the beauty of the meadows and lake below. I was reluctant to continue speaking of my professional life, for that must lead to the subject of my recent malaise, the burden of which I preferred not to impose on a stranger. But we conversed of many things besides, subjects high and low, and we had a grand time together, moving easily between solemnity and humor. After rejoining the path that ran through the meadow toward the village, I thanked him for the company and conversation, then headed back to my hotel. He for his part returned to the bench where we had met, bidding me goodbye until tomorrow, in case we should meet again, which he assured me he hoped we would do.

The rest of the day I remained indoors, and I managed to read and write productively for hours without pain. Later, after dinner, I prepared for my inaugural session at the sanatorium, scheduled for the following afternoon. I laid out a suit of clothes and canvas shoes for exercise, and a pair of linen shorts to wear in the baths. Then I washed my hands and face in the porcelain basin on the washstand and lay down to sleep. The next morning I awoke with the intention of studying before breakfast, but again I was driven to shut my books and close my eyes against a menacing migraine. An hour's rest dispelled the pain, and I fled the hotel to cool my head in the bracing alpine air. I did not however take my usual route toward the sanatorium grounds. I would visit the place later that very day, and, besides, I reckoned my chances of encountering my new acquaintance better by the lake. And I was right. I spied him as soon as I rounded the trees. He was sitting on his bench in the meadow beside the path, the little volume of Plato by his side.

I approached and bid the man good morning, and he in turn greeted me warmly, enthusiastically even. He was in good spirits, as I had come to expect of him, and again we walked together around the lake. Initially we spoke of many things, flowing from subject to subject; but in time he inquired about my presence in the valley. "For," he said, "I have spent a few summers here over the years, and I do not recall having seen you before. Am I right?"

I confirmed his observation, explaining that this was indeed my first occasion to visit. "I have come to take the cure," I said.

Although we had only just met, our conversation the previous day had somehow drawn us together. I was entirely at my ease in his company, and I sensed I could disclose to him even my most private thoughts. Therefore I proceeded to relate the facts of my situation, the strains of my professional life, my headaches and melancholia, my specific business at the sanatorium. He in turn listened empathetically, grimacing now and then, even confessed to having suffered kindred ailments in the past. Then, with reference specifically to my own headaches, he said, "Ah, well, all right, then. I suppose we shall have to treat you as a contemporary Charmides. No?"

I laughed at his joke, which really did surprise me, striking me not only as funny but apt. He laughed too and took my arm as we turned on the path that curved around the far shore of the lake.

"Now, I will not say I've recently been reading about you," he continued. "This volume I carry does not contain that compact little gem of a work. But if I may play the Socrates for just a moment, I believe I might possess a charm for your disorder. But to be certain of it, I propose we examine your condition more closely. If, that is, you have no objections."

I assured him I was willing to discuss the matter, which was true, for he had won me over utterly with his reference to Plato's *Charmides*. But for the benefit of those who are unacquainted with this dialogue, I should explain that early in the *Charmides* Socrates claims to have a healing charm to alleviate the headaches plaguing the eponymous central character of the work. The charm is no herb or potion, but rather certain "beautiful words," which is to say, apparently, the very conversation that is the content of the dialogue, the central topic of which is *sôphrosynê*, which we may translate as temperance or self-control. Socrates explains moreover that his charm must be applied directly to the soul, for, he

29

says, an unhealthy body cannot be healed independently of the soul.

With these facts in mind I expected my friend to subject me to a psychic dissection. And right I was, too, but his initial line of inquiry addressed my physiology. That is to say, he began by asking when last I'd suffered the *mal di testa*, and when I mentioned the pain I'd recently experienced while trying to study, he smiled and said, "Ah, well, yes, of course. And there we have it, don't we? But listen: even the ancient Charmides aspired to be a philosopher and a poet. Are you then content to be merely a scholar?"

The question took me aback. I had no idea what to make of it. Did he mean to attribute my headaches, and even my melancholia, to my being a scholar? I failed to see the connection, and I said as much in reply.

"Well," he explained, "the scholar is something of an unnatural kind, is he not? In any case, he certainly is at least a late-comer."

To this I replied, "I suppose that depends upon one's conception of lateness. For one might argue that the first great age of scholarship originated among the Alexandrians, which is to say among the ancients."

He not only accepted my point, he expanded on it, remarking that "one could even push the origin further back in time, back at least to Aristotle. You're right about that. But," he continued, and here he presented the gravamen of his case. "But what I mean to say, to state the matter crudely, is that the scholar is a parasite. Being small himself he feeds on the host of former greatness. Or, with the example of Aristotle now before us, we might say that the scholar is no self-mover. The creative man, the man whose life and work the scholar scrutinizes, placing him under the microscope of his myopia—this man, the poet, the philosopher, the artist, he alone is self-moving. The scholar by nature is inert, and he is set in motion by another, specifically by the active impetus deriving from the authentic originator, the prime mover, the poet or the philosopher. Is this not so?"

Here he turned to look me in the face, and in my expression I'm sure he read a tangle of agreement and repulsion, in my eyes a confusion of emotions.

"So this," he continued, perceiving that I was unprepared to speak, "this is what I mean by 'unnatural.' The scholar is less a natural kind than an offshoot, an outgrowth, a derivative type. Moreover, to return to Aristotle, since the nature of a thing—nature as *physis*, you understand—since nature is at bottom an internal principle of motion, which the scholar lacks, as I have said, he must then be unnatural in this sense as well. And of course I'm speaking now of the scholar *qua* scholar, not *qua* animal or human being."

With this he fell silent, and I reflected on his words while following our twinned reflection moving on the surface of the water. "I take your general point," I said. "Or anyway I think I do. But still I fail to see its bearing on my condition. I am after all quite satisfied with my scholarship."

"Oh, I'm sure you are," he replied. "I don't doubt it." He did not mean to question my contentment with my work, "but," he explained, "my worry is whether your life as lived moves you to exult in your being, in your being here and now. Satisfaction and scholarship are distinct from cheerfulness and life, no? A man might well be satisfied with his work but pained by the conditions of his existence, and the virtues of an industrious scholar can produce an inferior man. Or more to the point, the scholar's virtues might—and it is my contention that they do—inhibit the growth of the philosopher. And here I must ask you directly: is your life's aspiration to gather and collate information about the ancient lovers of wisdom, rather than to embrace the goddess yourself?"

As he put this final question to me we paused on the path, and he spread his arms expansively to encompass the totality of the landscape around us. Nature entire, but not simply as the world, the physical realm of established material being. Rather, nature as an ever-fertile upwelling multifariousness; a ceaseless flux of creative becoming; a manifold moving like water, self-diverse, surprising and forever fresh, forever new and renewed. This anyway is the impression his gesture made on me, my mind primed as it was by his provocative words, my own mutable mood, and the wild surrounding atmosphere.

As moved as I was, however, still I resisted the thrust of his argument; and I protested that in my life as a scholar I expressed the love I'd felt for the Greeks since my youth.

"Do you mean to tell me, then," he asked in reply, "that as a boy you cherished metrical analyses of Homer's hexameter and studies of Plato's use of particles? I must say I find this incredible. Were you not rather moved by Homer's savage beauty, Plato's creative profundities? And did you not fancy yourself in dreams an Achilles or a Socrates, or even a Homer or Plato remanifest? For surely a passion for the ancient poets and philosophers has never inspired a healthy child to imagine himself a scholar."

Of course he was right, and his words reminded me of my own youthful aspiration to inhabit a thought-world similar to Plato's. For years I'd longed to plumb the depths of Plato's character and mind, to excavate the hidden core of his creative intellectuality, and not for the sake of scholarly discovery or documentation, but rather to chart a course to a similar source of ideas and experiences within myself. University training had diverted my passion, however, and even my studies as a schoolboy had concentrated more on the mastery of grammatical minutiae than on cultivating my aesthetic or emotional sensitivities. Certainly I was never encouraged in school to nurture my own philosophical or artistic impulses, much less instructed how to do so.

This, he said, was precisely the point. "And of course this hasn't changed since you became a professor," he continued. "In fact, I'm sure your professional work has distanced you even further from every thought of developing your own intellectual and literary inclinations. The natural creative instincts that attract the authentically thoughtful mind to philosophy as a vocation are discouraged, even actively suppressed, through the training required to succeed in philosophy as a profession. And let's be frank and acknowledge the reality of the situation: the philosophy professor does not profess philosophy. He is a drone for pedantry, a book-man, a desk-man, a stunted and sallow lecturer. At best—or is this really worse?—the academic philosopher translates the genius of his great predecessors into conceptually precise terms, rearranging the revised propositions into formal arguments, then analyzing the results as to validity and soundness. And perhaps for a *soupçon* of creativity he cogitates for himself an implication of, or a counter-example to, the argument, which he then publishes as his own little contribution to the field, or sub-field, as the case may be—but at this point what does it matter, really? The stakes are so very low. Oh," he concluded with a flourish, "how our Plato must weep!"

We had come full circle around the lake, and as we turned onto the path that ran back through the meadow toward my friend's favorite bench and my hotel beyond, I remarked that "I suppose old Plato must weep indeed—if our situation really is so dire. And perhaps it is. But before I can agree in good conscience, I shall have to collect my thoughts."

I admit I was relieved we'd reached the natural terminus of our walk, for in the moment I had no coherent reply to his remarks. My head was swimming with ideas, but my thoughts were undeveloped vague impressions, isolated words and detached, dangling clauses. Therefore I suggested we continue our discussion the following morning. I needed time to think, I said, and, besides, it was time I return to my room to prepare for my appointment at the sanatorium.

My activities later at the spa were a refreshing change from my usual routine. The exercise did my body good—I hadn't stretched, strained, and leapt like that in years—and the healing waters of the hot-spring bath worked into my muscles and joints most soothingly indeed. The vegetarian meal was not at all to my taste, but later that evening I supplemented the nutritionist's roots and leaves with beef-stew, bread, and a large glass of red wine in a café beside my hotel. Later, before bed, I worked steadily for two full hours with no trace of pain; the ideas came easily and my writing flowed with clarity and precision. Immediately after I lay down to bed, however, my thoughts ran back to the morning's conversation, and although I slept, some small angle of my mind remained awake throughout the night talking, talking, talking. The following morning I rolled out of bed tired, and although I managed to work for a long stretch, in the back of my thoughts the monologue continued ceaselessly. Eventually I set aside my books and papers to dialogue with myself, hoping thus to clarify my position before speaking again with my challenging new friend.

I asked myself: What exactly had I been up to at my desk, surrounded by my books? Was I living as a philosopher or working as a professor? Or was I merely studying as a scholar? Such questions as these, and the further questions to which they in turn gave rise, formed the theme of my morning's ruminations.

After about an hour of this a knock at the door distracted me from my thinking, and I opened to find the morning attendant bearing a note from my friend suggesting that, since a cold drizzle was falling outside, we meet for coffee and conversation at the neighboring café. I arrived on the spot not twenty minutes later, and as I removed my overcoat I was greeted with a cry of, "*Buongiorno, caro* Charmides! *Eccomi qua!*" and I looked up to see my friend waving from a table beside a window in the back, the usual aura of mischief and solemnity dancing about his head.

After the waiter had taken our orders I recounted in brief my afternoon at the sanatorium. My friend put several questions to me regarding my experiences there, then eventually he asked whether I'd reflected on our conversation of the previous day. I had indeed, I said, both in the background of my dreams and after waking that morning. "Still," I added, "whether Plato weeps for me I cannot begin to imagine. In any case I doubt that my boyish naiveté is relevant to the matter at hand. One fantasizes as a child, to be sure. One plays the berserking warrior, hacking through the enemy's ranks with a branch for a sword; one chases the neighbor's pets and collapses in the mock agony of one's death-throes. But these are but juvenile games. Summer larks. Eventually one grows up, one matures. Surely you don't recommend I abandon my studies to run wild through town as if I were sacking Troy."

Of course I understood that he intended no such thing, but I was warming to my theme. Or perhaps I was only temporizing. In any case, eventually I carried on. "But as for my being a Homer or Plato," I said, "which I take to be your actual point, what can I say? There's no business in it. And I don't mean merely that one can't secure a salary—I mean to say there's no place in our world for this type of man. Ours is a prosaic age, an age of industry and commerce; and these days even the literary intellectual strives to secure his position among the bourgeoisie. Shall I revolt against this system? Shall I withdraw into the bohemian demimonde?

What good would it do me? None, I should think. And I rather expect it would do me grave harm.

"Think of it this way," I continued. "The academic life affords me the opportunity to pursue my passion for philosophy in a socially acceptable manner, I should say in even a respectable manner. It is, if you will, the responsible, adult expression of those youthful frivolities that were once, no doubt, entertaining, but which no serious man can sustain beyond his childhood. In short, then, I mean to say that the scholar's life is admirable, decent, and sensible. We are after all no longer children."

"Ah," my friend interjected, an arch expression brightening his face, "but on that last point you must speak for yourself, I'm afraid. But I shall hymn the virtues of the child some other time. For now I should make it clear that I acknowledge the prudence of life as you describe it. All due respect to prudence, of course, and honor too. Yet I must at the same time insist on the viability of a life beyond this. Even the superiority. Not a life of children's games, playing the hoplite with imaginary heroes. Of course not that! But, more to the point, I wonder whether as an academic you really do pursue your passion for philosophy. I suspect that what you call the responsible expression of this pursuit is actually a transformation so complete, so radical, as to amount to the abandonment of your passion.

"Consider the difference," he continued, "and the distance, between the philological study of a Platonic text and the rational analysis of Plato's arguments. Moreover—and this is the crucial point—neither of these activities is the sum of a life lived philosophically. Philological study and rational analysis may be elements of the philosophical life—in fact I am sure they are. But taken as ends in themselves—and, as you know, the perverse domain of academic professionalism promotes these things as the highest ends—taken thus they divert one's attention from philosophy to scholarship and logic. This is why the typical professor eventually abandons the love of wisdom for the calculus of practicality.

"In sum, then, I say that if your passion really ever was philosophy, it's likely that you *have* abandoned it. The scholar, the academic, the professor of philosophy is not a sensible philosopher. He is no philosopher at all."

"No philosopher?" I sighed, and this bare expression of surprise was the extent of my contribution.

"Yes, well, all right then," my friend carried on. "Permit me to explain. Now the following thought may not apply to other disciplines—the natural sciences, for instance—but as for philosophy, the profession tends to destroy the vocation. The virtues conducive to flourishing in the vocation—unbounded intellectual independence, reckless exploration, visionary leaps tempered by a bold skepticism, creative conceptual and linguistic expression—in short, thinking without limits—these virtues are suppressed by the requirements and routines of the profession.

"Having said this, however, I should stress that I don't mean to denigrate the value of scholarship altogether. Creativity devoid of expertise is vacuous—as expertise devoid of creativity is merely pedantic. Philosophy springs from the proper intermingling of artistry and knowledge. Substance and style. Matter and form. And above all, *life,* abundant and overflowing. Yes, as I have just suggested, the philosopher must be—or at least it's best if he once has been—a scholar, but he must become much more than this. He must master the skills of scholarship without the discipline mastering him. But this is no easy undertaking. The effort requires so much time and concentrated dedication that over the years, and by imperceptible degrees, the average young academic eventually adopts the scholar's modes of evaluation, including of course the thought that the scholar's life is in some decisive respect superior to the philosopher's. Then, my friend—ah, well, then it's all over with the love of wisdom, and no aspiration higher than the accumulation of knowledge remains."

At this point he paused and looked at me closely, narrowing his eyes. Then, after a moment of tense silence, he relaxed and continued.

"Listen," he said, "Plato's Charmides suffered from his own peculiar problems, much different from yours, no doubt. Whether he sincerely aspired to philosophy and poetry or was only blustering to impress his fellows, I can't say. But either way, in the end his lust for power and pleasure destroyed him. His headaches may well have been no more than the inevitable consequence of his debauchery. But his fundamental flaw was that he did not know himself, or rather that he didn't even care to try."

Here I nodded my agreement.

"And how about you, my friend?" he asked. "I have been thinking of you, evaluating your condition, on the assumption that philosophy is more to you than a profession, that some part of you, deep down, craves to live philosophy rather than merely to study it. But am I right? Only you can make this determination—if, that is, you really know yourself. Head pains alone could have a purely physiological aetiology, but together with bouts of melancholy I suspect a psychosomatic source. But, as I say, I must leave the final diagnosis up to you."

I knew my friend was right, of course. Right not only about the possible diagnoses, but also in his specific analysis. My problem likely was psychosomatic, certainly at least for the most part. I hadn't tended responsibly to my physical health over the years; and perhaps I'd been even more neglectful of my psychic well-being. Even so I was not convinced that the root of my malady was that my scholarly pursuits suppressed my philosophical drive. Therefore as he finished speaking I thought less about his concluding remarks concerning my condition than his dismissal of "the accumulation of knowledge." It was evident that he'd meant to distinguish knowledge from wisdom. But this made no sense to me, and I said so.

"Wait," I said, "let's go back a minute. If I heard you correctly, and I believe I did, you implied that wisdom and knowledge are somehow distinct. Was this really your intention? But this can't be right, can it?"

He made no reply to my question, but only smiled his arch smile, and his eyes again gleamed mischievously.

"No," I answered for him. "This cannot be right. For does not the way to wisdom run along the road of truth?"

His face now shone more brightly. He leaned forward.

"And does one not proceed along this road by accuracy of interpretation guided by objective analysis, which is to say, in a word, by way of knowledge? Of course one does! One walks the road to wisdom by seeking and knowing truth. We have understood this since Parmenides, father of logic, master of knowledge!"

Now a look of delighted surprise passed over his face, prompted by my discernment or my folly I could not tell.

"In short, then," I concluded, in a tone intended to communicate definitiveness, "wisdom is by definition the possession of certain knowledge of objective truth. Surely. I am only paraphrasing Aristotle here, from whose analysis I infer that the sage is preeminently a knower, the wise man one who knows the truth. Of this at least I have no doubt."

My friend sat back in his chair, and I read from his expression that my appeal to certainty had not moved him. I suppose it didn't help that as I spoke my head began to ache, and that my pain was apparent from my having to massage my forehead. For his part, my interlocutor was utterly relaxed, only the pulsing of his right temple hinted at the whirring of his mind. He leaned forward again, laid his palms on the table, and addressed me with his customary tone of genial seriousness.

"Well, friend Charmides," he said, "that your mind is wholly untainted by doubt is clear from the zeal with which you express yourself. Very good. But whether your expression manifests a passion for philosophy is another question. But I see now that we shall have to pursue these matters at a deeper level, and I shall have to apply my charm to your overestimation of the value of truth."

Then rising from his seat he smiled and said, "But let us put this off to another day. It will not be easy work; we shall have to prepare ourselves. Besides, since the clouds at last have exhausted their supply of rain, and the sun peeks through their dispersing ranks, we'd do well I think to treat ourselves to the uncommon joy of a contemplative stroll around the lake."

III

Divine Madness

My head ached terribly as I left the meeting to which I'd been summoned by representatives of the Senior Administration. Officials at every level of the institutional hierarchy had been "hurt and angered" by the note I'd sent condemning their vision of our university, as I have previously mentioned. Yet they were in no position to dismiss me. My reputation in my field was such that they had need of me, if only to exploit my name for their own advantage. They could, however, reprimand me, make me suffer for my "impudence," my "perversity" and "lack of community spirit," and it was implied (very nearly declared outright) that I should expect as much.

As angry as my superiors were, they could not match my own rage. Theirs was the frustration of a dominant power unable to subdue every non-compliant will, no matter how insignificant, or how righteous. They would break even a butterfly on their wheel. My own temper was the fiery issue of indignation struck against exasperation. My colleagues and I understood the history of education in the West; we cherished the university as a cultural institution; and we were trained to transmit traditions of learning from generation to generation, each of us a link in a chain stretching centuries into the past, the binding line of civilization. Yet we were subject to a compound force alloyed of several petty autocrats, each individually ignorant and insubstantial, but as a collective reinforced by the final power in our world today, capital.

Beyond the bureaucracy that dominated the university, and thereby indirectly much of my life, was the broader culture, as boorish as even the most philistine member of the university Board. And so insistent too. The hectic commotion of citizens at their puerile pursuits was everywhere unavoidable, especially since, as diverse as their particular passions were, they evidently had in common one and the same secondary interest, namely, the desire to persuade their fellows to share their every personal enthusiasm. Every man a hawker of his own ego. Moreover, it was precisely around this time that business began to grasp the power of perverting patrons into living advertisements. Convince the public that corporate imprints are a mark of status, and mindless mobs of materialistic dupes will eagerly aspire to display their allegiance to the fashionable brands of the day, thereby serving unwittingly as unsalaried promotional flacks.

Socrates told his Athenian jurors that the Olympic victor made them merely think that they were happy, whereas he made them really be happy. These days it seems there are only aspiring Olympians and their mobs of squawking admirers. Not a single Socrates among them, much less a Plato. More and more we lose ourselves in appearances, including of course the illusion that we have finally found the real.

Such were the thoughts bedeviling me as I plodded home through the snow from school, stewing over the crude disingenuousness of my superiors, contemptuous of the two-bit merchants and drone-consumers scurrying about the city center. But perhaps I should pause at this point to note, lest I alienate my readers, that I know full well I exaggerate my censure of the world beyond myself to the point of being obnoxious, also to acknowledge my own participation in the cultural corruptions I denounce. I recognized my complicity even at the time of the events I recount in this narrative, but in those days my anger drove me to extremes and I couldn't help myself.

The truth is I was sorely disappointed with the world around me, more specifically with the time into which I'd been born. I couldn't help but think, for example, that had the Italian Renaissance proceeded along its natural course, its roots so deep in ancient soil, Europe might well have been purified of the baser elements in Christianity without succumbing to the rationalist French Enlightenment and its crude utilitarian appropriation by the Brits. In that case our specific here and now would be much different, and much better, or so it seemed to me. Our reason leavened with Hermetic mysteries, myth, and magic; our knowledge a brother to our dreams.

To this day I long to escape into another era, a past century. (I have no interest in the future, which according to the popular imagination will be but a sleek, ultra-modern, intensified version of contemporary nonsense.) An irrational desire, I know, but at the time of my story in particular I experimented with irrationality as a mode of liberation, of deliverance and release. I went out of my way to lose myself exploring every corridor in the labyrinth of madness.

Conversation and correspondence with my friend over the years had encouraged me to pursue a new mode of life. His own manner of being in the world inspired me to live authentically as a philosopher, and to conceive the type as a creative-intellectual spirit distinct from, and superior to, the scholar and professional academic. Yet still my thoughts on the theme were less expansive than his, my relation to philosophy impersonal and abstract. Between the time of our initial meeting, when I had only just begun my career, and the later post-war period, I had liberated my long-suppressed aspiration to live an authentically philosophical life, yet I could see no way to manage it. Hence my dissatisfaction, my frustration and rage. Hence also my occasional craving for madness.

According to my own analysis, of myself and of my times, my intellectual and existential potentialities were constrained by the time and place of my birth. I had inherited assumptions and structural beliefs that imprisoned me in walls of thought which I had no part in designing. I matured intellectually in an era of the most extreme, and most naive, empiricism and materialism, a positivist period which taught that science alone provides access to the truth. And by science I mean a disciplined study, focused on a field of natural kinds, grounded on evidence acquired through research or observation, adhering to a systematic methodology, proceeding by way of experimentation and the dispassionate analysis of data, and with conclusions justified by appeal to objective criteria. In short, the *Wissenschaften*, from philology to physics. (I set aside for now the complication that science thus defined is a theoretical construct with no counterpart in reality.)

I say that I was "taught" to believe in science as the sole arbiter of reality and truth, but really these days one absorbs positivism through cultural osmosis, long before one's proper education begins, and even if one's family is devout. Religious beliefs are considered a matter of personal faith, private, eccentric, epistemically dubious, and in general they are shunted off to a region of the mind—or, better, the heart—wholly disconnected from one's thoughts about the world.

Philosophers and theologians from Plato to Aquinas argued that the metaphysical (call it the "supernatural" if you like) is intelligible, a proper object of knowledge. But certain branches of Protestantism and early modern philosophy and science formed an alliance against this ancient understanding. From their opposite ends of the spiritual spectrum they insisted that only the physical world is knowable; the metaphysical—its essential nature, of course, but even its very existence—is at best only credible, a matter of belief, or of faith. But in a world of mechanized industry and technology, of concrete artifacts conspicuous to the senses and ceaselessly impinging on the body, material things seem so obviously real that nebulous objects of faith tend by comparison to lose a measure of their presumed actuality, until over time they drift away into the realm of the fantastic and the foolish. Thus do items formerly regarded as realities known by the rational degenerate into fictions only wished for by the deluded.

But my point has less to do with specifically religious modes of thought than with every variety of conception beyond the scope of a reductively rationalist account of intellect and a materialist ontology. Consider Parmenides, Heraclitus, Aeschylus, Sophocles, Plato, Plutarch, Dante, Michelangelo, Pico, Giordano Bruno, and William Blake: who today can inhabit their thought-worlds, so full of mystery, magic, art, science, reality, dreams, visions, fact, and symbol all at once? Who today would want to, conditioned as we are to regard such men as quaint, ignorant, aberrant, or delusional? It's as though we require the permission of the natural sciences even to entertain a thought.

So, as I say, this is the world into which I was born. By the time I was introduced to knowledge and belief, truth and falsehood, being and becoming, I was primed to adopt unquestioningly the standard intellectual presumptions of modernity, as if together they formed the bedrock of the unconditioned human standpoint. In short, my philosophical imagination was constricted by historical contingencies which acted on me—or, rather, operated in me—as natural necessities. I could not plumb the depths of Plato's mind even if I wanted to. And at times I did want to, eagerly. But between the ideas that moved me most profoundly and those I was able to "believe" there yawned an unbridgeable abyss.

There are times I suspect that the problem I mean to identify here is less an issue of one's capacity to believe, as a matter of pure intellectual possibility, than of the sort of beliefs one's surroundings incline one to accept. An ancient thinker wandering at leisure in the open air of nature had easy access to a conceptual field rich and inexhaustible. He could believe in gods, in atoms, in tragedy, in nature, in war as the father and king of all, in the Delphic pythia and the mystery traditions of Dionysus. The harried denizen of a modern city cramped with man-made objects is more or less restricted to the human things, to the material and artificial. In this connection we might say that a meadow or a mountain was the world's first temple, and that an urban-scape of asphalt, steam, and steel is the copestone on the edifice of disenchantment.

Now, tell me, what resolution can there be of this predicament but madness? One longs to break the bonds of spiritual confinement, to sneak out of one's own mind, so narrow, so limited and limiting. And the infuriating social constraints! Quite apart from the desire for liberation from a prosaic rationality, one yearns for frankness against the lies of mass culture, against the sophistry of political popinjays and the decadence of intellectuals. Even an infusion of creative fabrication, the freedom of untamed fantasy, is preferable to the realm of mindless labor, shallow spectacle, and unreflective opinion we've elaborated for ourselves, or, I should say, *against* ourselves. Who is alive, alive and thinking, and feeling, in this ridiculous wasteland of mind-and soul-death?!

> *Burn it down: It's a pity that after a rush of exuberance or rage one doesn't burst into flame and disappear.*

I wrote this in my notebook walking home from school, my thoughts twisting, choler rising, forehead hot despite the snow, and pounding. I reread the note on entering my study and sitting at my desk. Still in something of a frenzy, I traced the lines over again in pencil, darkening and deepening the strokes. The letters glowed and gave off heat. The words scorched the page. My mind boiled. Come, O madness, my salvation!

As eager as I often was to effect an ecstatic displacement of self from mind, I knew full well that the madman is no philosopher. The insane are neither free spirits nor free thinkers; their ravaged spirits don't think at all, or anyway not deeply, and their thoughts are warped by their disorder. At any rate they discover no communicable profundities, lost as they are in their mists of dim confusion. True, in our more romantic moods we sometimes fancy that madmen achieve a psychic state so far removed from this world, slipping into a blissful realm of ineffable truth, that they voluntarily disengage from the frivolous obsessions and delusions that harass us ordinary mortals. But this, as I say, is but romantic fancy. The mad are in touch with no truth, nor do they have a choice in the matter of their condition.

I understood all this. Nevertheless, the facts did not consistently impress me as relevant. An imprisoned man, despairing, may be moved to resort to radical schemes to break the chains that bind him, from dissolution of the self to the throttling of his captor, even if only in his fantasies. But this is all just so much wasted effort, energy expended to no good end.

True salvation is obtainable, but the secret thereto is concealed within a curved mirror, and the mode of discovery involves an intricate decentering of vision.

Deliverance issues from a certain kind of madness, to be sure, but human madness is only its distorted image. The authentic look of madness is reflected in the archaic smile etched into the mask of a god.

Plato in the *Phaedrus* writes that the greatest of goods come to men through god-given madness, which is, he adds, superior not only to human madness but even to human sanity and self-control. The philosophical life expresses the highest form of divine madness, the philosopher being possessed by Eros. Moved in particular by the sight of beauty, the philosopher experiences a "divine release from customary usages," liberation from the normal ways of men. And thus "withdrawing from human pursuits" he adopts new modes of living and thinking. He becomes a philosopher, his attention turned toward manifestations of the divine. For this he is reproached by the many as if he were disturbed, for it escapes them that he is in fact possessed by a god.

This theme recurs in the *Phaedo*, in which the philosopher's "release" is depicted as a living separation of the soul (or mind) from the body, a process known as *katharsis*, or purification. Which brings us back to the empiricism and materialism I mentioned earlier in connection with positivism. In the *Phaedo* Plato denounces as "the greatest and most extreme of all base things" the beliefs, often conjoined, that visible objects are manifest and true—a formulation of the empiricists' doctrine that knowledge is acquired only through the senses—and that those things are true which the body declares to be so—which in context amounts to the materialists' doctrine that physical objects alone exist. The philosopher avoids or overcomes this crude positivist dogma through the practice of purification, which is to say through the separation of soul from body, which in the *Phaedrus* Plato describes as the withdrawal of attention from human things and ascribes to divine madness.

I don't claim that my longing for madness was consistently motivated by a desire to live as a Platonist, not anyway as this type has been represented by the tradition. I wasn't exactly always seeking knowledge of the Forms, likeness to God, or unification with the One. But neither do I admit that traditional dogmatic Platonism expresses the philosophic spirit of Plato himself. We mustn't confuse Platonism the metaphysical-ethical system with Plato the philosopher-artist. Besides, sometimes I was after a Rimbaudian derangement of the senses having nothing directly to do with either Platonism or Plato. And to this end I turned to an altogether different breed of deity, Dionysus.

Ah, yes, god of the vine, in my glass, in my blood and brain. In the kitchen I filled a small carafe and returned with it and a tumbler to my study. I drank while thumbing through my notebook, my heated thoughts still swirling around the frustrations of my job, the preposterous masquerades of mass culture, and the devious constraints that stifled the autonomy of my intellect.

Since adolescence I'd been a drinker of red wine, initiated into the enchantments of the tavern by my father. I'd given it up in the immediate aftermath of his death, but soon I was worshiping once again at the ivied altar of

Bacchus, sacrificing my lucidity for visions and insight in return.

Dionysus is a manifold divinity, depicted variously by the ancients as anthropomorphic and as a marauding bull; as a bearded elder and an effeminate youth; as a bringer of delight and a holy terror; as a relief from care and a source of troubled anxiety; as immortal and as slain, dismembered, and resurrected; as a channel of birth and a goad to murder; as a bright Olympian and a chthonic idol of the under-world—in short, as a god symbolic simultaneously of life, peace, and cheerfulness, and of death, violence, and mad-ness. And so it is with the bounty of his beneficence, wine. The god's great blooming vine is nourished by the secret founts of generation and destruction, joy and grief, serenity and disorder. Its roots are sunk in heaven and hell, its fruit sprouts ripe in both realms. Hence the drinking man, infused with a Dionysian potency, is mellow or inflamed, he is a lover or a street-fighter, a wise man or a fool.

As god of the grape and of vegetation generally, of fertility and sex, associated in particular with women and wild animals, with ecstasy, music, dance, and tragedy, Dionysus is both a nature deity and a patron of human artifice. And he is thereby moreover a god of paired opposites, of harmony in tension. In the Bacchic rites we encounter just such juxtaposed oppositions—of, for example, life-death, peace-war, truth-falsehood—as we find in the obscure pronouncements of Heraclitus. Dionysus, then, is also a mystic and a philosopher.

As an aspirant to philosophy myself, philosophy as a way of life rather than as a discipline or profession, I often joined the retinue of Dionysian revelers, as I have said. I drank not only to submerge dark moods but also toward the end of intellectual exploration. Dionysian intoxication tends to induce the feeling of power and the freedom from mundane cognitive constraints which together are generative of art. Not merely art as artifact, but art as insight, creative insight, the power of the philosopher-artist to evoke new perspectives and novel thought-worlds from out of voids of darkness.

At the conclusion of Plato's *Symposium*—in which Socrates appears as a prodigious drinker—the drunken Alcibiades refers to the "madness and Dionysian frenzy of the philosopher." And in the *Phaedrus* Socrates associates the lover of wisdom with the lover of beauty, also with the *erotikos*, the erotic man, and the *mousikos*, committed to the arts over which the Muses preside. Among such arts we may include non-mimetic poetry, and in the *Phaedrus* and elsewhere Plato writes of the poet as one who is inspired, mad, and possessed by a Dionysian frenzy. Taking these passages together with the example of Plato himself—author of one among the peak-supreme artistic achievements in the history of the West—we might identify the philosopher with the poet as a free-spirited, exploratory, creative-intellectual artist, as, in short, a disciple of the philosopher Dionysus.

There are times I believe, or anyway I like to imagine, that even God (or whatever one should call the metaphysical source of physical reality, assuming there is such a thing) is such a Dionysian creative-intellectual artist. A theme runs through the mystical branches of the Platonic tradition according to which our spatial-temporal world of physical plurality is but the phenomenal expression of the self-reflective activity of the non-spatial, non-temporal, immaterial One, the appearance of itself to itself under the guise of space, time, and causality. The deity's act of knowing brings this world into being, or, more accurately, its act of knowing just *is* the being of this world. In short, when God, or the One, contemplates itself, it knows itself as this world, as me, for example, observing the world around me. My body is but a mode of God's activity, my mind a mode of the deity's self-consciousness. As I say, this idea appeals to me, at least in my more mystical moods. But even when I'm in such a mood I modify the standard account, according to which the divine is solely an agent and object of knowledge, to include among its self-reflective activity imagination, fantasy, mythologizing, self-deception, speculation, longing, playfulness and jest. And since the One as creative-intellectual artist is unconditioned and unbound, the resulting world of art, philosophy, science, dream, melancholy, fantasy, exuberance, and rage never exhausts itself. There is no end of history.

No *final* end. For, to return to the human realm, the power of Dionysian intoxication can generate more than even the creative insight of the philosopher-artist. It can bring an end to the man himself, as it were. The ritual reveler infused with the spirit of the ecstatic god may be liberated altogether from the bonds of the *principium individuationis*, the principle of individuation, which constrains the human mind to experience the world under the aspect of space and time, through the activity of which the

All is divided into distinct and discrete particulars. In the Dionysian experience these categories evaporate, and with them goes the individual too. Temporarily he vanishes from God's eternal self-reflective reverie. His experience no longer bound by space and time, his very being no longer manifesting spatial-temporal properties, the furious Dionysian sinks into the eternal flux of Becoming, is dissolved and swept away.

This disunion and dispersal of the self, utter dissolution, was at times my singular goal. Systematic derangement not only of the senses but of the intellect and the person too. To exist no longer as a body, soul, or mind, but to burst the bonds of the human frame and to scatter as a surge, a spray, an insubstantial mist of free-floating chemical compounds, or an infinitely expanding range of dissociated particles, waves on an oscillating field, or the undifferentiated continuum of energy circulating at, and as, the fundament of the sphere of materiality. In short, when seized by passions of exhilarated joy or anger I longed to dissociate from myself so thoroughly as to be everything and nothing, to erupt, to explode, to disperse and radiate. Not to die, mind you. Rather I aimed to be a living multiplicity distinguished by a unity of vision.

Of course none of this was possible. Formerly maybe, among the ancients immersed in cultic ritual. But no more, and certainly not through drunkenness alone. The closest I've come is in moments of enraptured immersion in nature. For example, in the course of certain inspired days hiking in the mountains in the years following my initial visit and the first meetings with my friend. A profoundly transformative potency pervades the alpine atmosphere, its power enhanced by an ambience resonant with a life-force which I shall designate, for lack of a better word, divine. Plato was familiar with the phenomenon. In the *Phaedrus* he conducts his Socrates beyond the city walls into the natural world, lays him down on soft grass, in the shade of a fragrant tree, barefoot beside a splashing stream. As disinclined as Socrates is to remove himself from the urban center, he admits that the area strikes him as divine. The place is sacred to Pan and the Nymphs, nature deities all, and Socrates later remarks that the divinity of the place infuses him with a divine pathos, that he is even on the verge of being possessed by the Nymphs' mania. He had thought that he could learn only from "men in the city," but Plato suggests that "rural areas and the trees" can teach the philosopher the deepest of lessons, presumably through the madness inspired by their natural beauty.

My friend once remarked that he loves mountain valleys with eyes, by which he meant with lakes. The image stays with me as a figure of nature personified, deified, of earth gazing into sky as a god contemplating the contents of its own mind, the clouds overhead its fleeting thoughts, conceptions gathering, shifting, and dispersing, the whole enlivened by the sun as the generative energy of creative intellect ceaselessly bringing forth new life.

Therefore I say that Plato was right, and madness really is a gift from the gods—*if* we conceive of nature, not literally as a divinity, but rather as symbolic of a passage to a state beyond the mundanely human. In this case the look of madness in the smile of a god would flash from the laughing eyes of alpine lakes absorbed in the self-reflective act of nature observing nature thinking nature, an infinite regress of earth, water, air, and fire, beauty perpetually multiplied.

Now imagine a sensitive pondering man set down in such a place. Quiet or clamorous, relaxed or frenetic—is he not mad? Yes, he is. He must be. For the gods take hold of such men abroad alone in the wild, and caught up in the divine grip they are mad as lovers of beauty, as *erotikoi* and *mousikoi*, and thereby are they also mad as lovers of wisdom, as philosophers.

I imagined such a man—my friend as he was, myself as I longed to be—as I emptied the carafe into my glass and crossed my study to stand beside the window. The sight of falling snow chilled my skin despite the alcohol boiling in my blood. Colder still was the realization that for all the apparent tranquility of the scene outside, beyond my small garden, and just beneath the layers of ice, the cacophonous artificialities of the modern world endured, and even the few remaining stands of natural vegetation had long since been subdued, hemmed in, rationally redesigned and engineered to serve utilitarian ends. I thought: It's true, alas, the great god Pan is dead.

The disadvantage of being a god is that if you happen to die, there may exist no other divinity of a power sufficient to resurrect you. And if God is dead, then we humans will have to confront alone the challenge of identifying the motivation and means to surpass ourselves as we are. For if nothing is real beyond the human sphere, to what higher condition may we reasonably aspire? And here we circle back to the theme of unreason as a mode of liberation from the constraints imposed on the mind's free movement by historical and cultural contingencies. If philosophy is not strictly divine, still the philosopher who seeks more than employment or a reputation must strive to be somehow other than conventionally human.

My own approach to this predicament was to devise and explore novel modes of thinking and perceiving, bold new forms of life and expression. But although I could imagine, dream, or hallucinate such spiritual innovations, I could not live them, or I could carry into life and action only their pale images. This was the one intolerable thing. The limitations of the real constantly chagrined me. Hence the necessity of madness, the warping or outright annihilation of the cognitive *a priori*, revolt from modern bourgeois strictures on imagination and action, and the imperative to resist the prevailing perversion according to which the nature of the philosopher is exhausted in the person of the scholar, the academic, the professor of philosophy. Hence, in short, my desire, not to solve a mystery, but to create one, in myself and of myself.

IV

Hard Fate and Black Bile

This world is such a dastardly place, and life so damnably hard, that perhaps we should grant to everyone the liberty to live as they see fit.

So one thinks from time to time, and a noble thought it is too. The imagination of those who cannot entertain the possibility is no doubt impoverished. Yet noble as it is, this idea runs up against the insight that some ways of life lead almost inevitably to ruin, even from the point of view of the man who lives as he sees fit. From this then comes the impulse to evaluate, judge, advise, implore, and prescribe—to children, for example. And from this in turn originate laws pertaining even to adults, if only to prevent them harming the young through their pernicious example. In this way liberty and law are tangled up in endless cycles of conflict, and there is no final resolution.

And here we have an instance of life's being hard, which brings us back to our original thought...

I wrote the above in my notebook aboard a train on the day I departed the Val di Sogno, earlier than I'd intended, summoned to my father's deathbed.

I had not seen my father in many years, and I'm not sure I knew for certain where he was. But three weeks into my stay in the mountains I received a letter which prompted me to curtail my visit to tend to him. I would have to take the cure another time, and my friend and I postponed our conversations. The latter fact distressed me far more than the former. Regarding my father's plight, I don't know quite how I felt. I suppose I was ambivalent. He had brought his ill health on himself, yet had he been born into a world more suited to his nature, he may well have flourished.

My father's father farmed the lowlands between the Greisler and the Little Nettle which has no name but which the locals refer to as the "Moss-Pines." The twenty hectares of land had been in the family since the middle of the eighteenth century, and its fertile and abundant soil sustained generations of my ancestors. Of course they suffered the occasional season of hardship from drought or heavy rains, but they always recovered in time. Yet this cycle of good fortune came to an end with the so-called "Century Floods" of the late-70s, two years of rainstorms relieved by only irregular breaks during the summer months. In the autumn of '78 the peril was such that my grandfather abandoned the land altogether, and when he concluded the following summer that the waters would never recede, that the rivers' banks and courses had been permanently distorted, he migrated to the city.

My father was still a boy at the time; he must have been seven or eight years old. Having been reared as a simple child of nature, he was uprooted and grafted onto the city. No, not grafted—a metaphor drawn from the natural world—but rather affixed, as if welded, or nailed, artifact to artifact. From the plow to the Pullman; from meandering paths to gridded avenues; from stars to gas-lamps, flowers to fashion, free play to the burden of alienating labor. I'm sure the relocation and consequent existential reorientation traumatized him. How could it not have done? Besides, one of my great-aunts once told me as much.

My father was born to live outdoors. God had intended him for a farmer. Yet evidently the deity also willed that his farmland should be destroyed, flooded and lost forever. So, well, I don't know what to make of that. Perhaps the divine is nothing like we have been taught to believe. Perhaps there is no God. In any case, my father was brought to the city, and there he suffered. He wandered through his days as if he'd been displaced and was pining for his natural home. As a child he regularly tramped the mile to the city limits and roamed the meadows and woods beyond, picking flowers and climbing trees, wading through streams and swimming in ponds, singing along with the birds, napping in the grass beneath nomadic clouds. I'm told there were occasions my grandfather had to go out at night to find him and bring him home. It was as if he were tracking an animal escaped into the wild when the poachers who'd captured the beast admitted it could not be tamed. But my father was no wild animal, however much he might have longed to live as one. He was human, and the human animal, alas, is easily broken.

My father was blessed with a natural talent for working with his hands, and in the summer of his tenth year his father enrolled him as apprentice to a master smith of the family's acquaintance. As a friend the man was the only master in the region willing to abide the boy's frequent absences and absent-mindedness. He trained him whenever he turned up and let him be when he didn't. He had other young apprentices to perform the necessary chores, and he reasoned that my father would be no use when lost in one of his "nature moods."

As sporadic as were my father's efforts to learn his craft, he was blessed with the intuitive spirit that guided him instinctively through a recapitulation of the stages magician, alchemist, metallurgist, apprentice, and master of the smithy. His combination of natural talent and acquired skills carried him well beyond his peers. It was evident even from his youth. Over the years he produced all manner of articles, from simple nails and hand-tools to such larger and more intricate works as the gears for water-wheels and various components of the movements of tower-clocks. His every piece was a work, not merely of craft, but of art. Observing the best of his productions one caught a glimpse of the abysmal difference between the absurdly cognate "ingenuity" and "genius." A miniature pulley-and-gear mechanism, which he cast from iron and coated in brass, a masterful execution, was for years displayed under glass in the city-hall of a nearby town. When the object disappeared, a rumor went round that a visiting collector had absconded with it under his cloak. Who knows whether this is so, but I would not be surprised to learn that the rumor is true.

Everyone in our region who had need of a smith thought immediately of my father, not least because, as skilled as he was, and as in demand, his services were affordable. Indeed, often when his work intrigued or delighted him he refused payment altogether. However persistently his customers pressed him, he declined with a smile or sneaked off when they left him unattended. Usually he insisted that conversation during his breaks was sufficient compensation, for the man loved to talk, which to him at times was a mode of musing and dreaming aloud. The grace of a poet suffused his spirit. This no doubt contributed to the artistry that informed his craft, and it manifested also in the rolling flow of his speech. When inspired he spoke as if nature herself were disclosing her private meditations through the rhythm of his words.

All this is to say that my father was something of a late-born Romantic. Unfortunately, although his poetic sensibility made him an object of admiration, a wonder to the farmers, laborers, and clerks among whom he moved, his eccentricities contributed to an irregular and unstable existence. I have just mentioned his often refusing payment for his labor. Worse than this was the fact that he worked only intermittently, only when the spirit moved him. Much of his time he filled, as he had done in his youth, roaming through the open spaces between the hamlets, villages, and towns of our region. When the weather was warm and dry, he slept outdoors and bathed in natural springs or streams. In winter he sometimes returned home to stay in his father's house, which the old man left to his sisters—my father's aunts—when he concluded that his son had no intention of settling into the routine required to maintain it. Some winters, however, he didn't turn up at all, and to this day I have no idea where he stayed. I suspect my mother didn't either, for they fell out not long before I started to school, and even when I spent time with him, she had little use for the man.

As a child I mostly accompanied my father on his roving "nature walks." We crisscrossed the meadow-lands together, explored the local forests and hiked up into the mountains, my father commenting all the while on the native flora, the trees and wildflowers in particular, noting their seasonal alterations and complex interconnections, one species to the other, to the insects and animals that shared their habitat, and to the broader ecology of our region, our state, our continent. He interrupted his discourses only to break into exuberant song or, alternatively, to curse the encroachments of the steadily expanding townships.

When I was older, though I saw my father less often, I learned of his one reconciliation to urban life: the tavern. In his company I came to appreciate the pleasures of drink. In doing so I realized the other cause of his wayward life, and of my mother's disappointment, not to say her animosity.

It would be unfair to call my father a drunkard, but he did enjoy lounging in his cups. I believe the distracted light-headedness elevated him above the melancholy he experienced from the impracticability of a productive natural life. As I have said, he was born to work a farm, to cultivate the land; but he was cast into a world in which the spread of homogenous fabrications was displacing nature's idiosyncratic art. He drank to forget the brutishness, or at least temporarily to reconcile himself to it.

My father was not an angry drinker; he harbored no latent bitterness. To the contrary, the alcohol often enkindled his finer poetic sensibilities. His melancholy touched, and thereby lightened, by the intoxicating flame, his heart quickened and tongue loosened, the whole of his being suffused with an aesthetic rush—the result was a flow of mellifluous sentiment which rapt the attention of our bar-mates. On such occasions my father could move a crowd to tears of merriment or sorrow, or both in alternating waves, and those who happened to be also acquainted with the artistry of his handiwork looked on him then with astonished admiration, tinged with sympathy, as if he were a force of nature subdued by the might of man but retaining a sad magnificence.

I recall an evening after one such a performance. The both of us were more or less impaired, to put the matter delicately. Moreover, the hour was late and we were a good long walk from my mother's house, in a neighboring village in fact. We sang as we exited the tavern, my father descending from the heights of his earlier jocularity, I attempting to distract myself from our predicament:

> The yellow daisy, so like the sun,
> She makes of our meadow a sky.
> Oh, why must you fade as the seasons run,
> In flight from the moon's pale eye?

My father had improvised the melody and lyrics when I was a boy. We sang the song whenever we walked together outdoors, warm in the morning sun, dewy hills lambent on the horizon, waist-high stalks of chicory blooming beside the river bank in wide lavender bands.

But to return to my reminiscence: we made our way singing through a maze of alleys and lanes, my father directing our steps until we drew up before a door on which he knocked in a distinctive rhythmic pattern. Soon a woman appeared, and seeing my father she smiled as if she'd expected him. Then she let us in. As I stumbled over the threshold the woman took me around the shoulders and set me in a chair beside a diminishing fire, then embracing my father's waist and whispering in his ear, she led him into an adjacent room. I must have fallen asleep there and then, for I awoke in the morning to my father shaking me gently by the arm. He asked me to bury the embers in the hearth with ash, and to be quiet about it, then he slipped out the front door. When he returned he carried a bundle of hand-picked wild-flowers which he arranged in a vase on a table by the door. The pungency of their sweet aroma struck me as we left, stepping lightly, moving in silence, my father's finger to his lips. To this day the unprompted recurrence of this scent returns me to that moment, quiet in the morning haze, the muffling mystery of secret passions and plans. Walking through the awakening fields toward my mother's house, the pale red sun rising at our backs, we sang and spoke of many things, but my father made no mention of the woman in whose home we'd passed the night.

This was the last such adventure I recall experiencing with my father. I rarely saw him after leaving home to attend university. Busy as I was with my studies, I did not often return to town; and he receded further into a solitary life. It may be that he drank more often, and more excessively. I saw him once through the window of a train when returning home for holiday. He sat in a meadow with his back to a tree, napping, or day-dreaming, or lost in hazy recollections of his youth, a half-eaten apple in the grass beside him. He appeared unwell, disheveled, unshaven and thin. I sallied out to look for him several times over the course of the week, but to no avail. I believe that glimpse from the train was the last time I laid eyes on him until I visited him in the hospital.

My father was not especially old, but he had lived a hard life, and his body showed the signs. He was conscious when I arrived to see him, but I could not tell whether he recognized me. He could barely speak, and when he tried to vocalize, his words were slurred beyond all understanding. Sitting down beside him I leaned in close and spoke directly into his ear, told him who I was and that I loved him, that he had been brought to hospital but that I was with him and would stay until he recovered. He seemed to try to smile and he squeezed my hand, a sign of recognition and comprehension, as I wanted to believe. I sat with him throughout the afternoon, alternately consulting with his doctor and reminding him of my presence. I spoke at length of our walking tours, described his favorite landscapes. Before I left I assured him once again that I, his son, was with him, and that I loved him, and that although I had to go I would return early the next day.

On my way to the hospital the following morning it occurred to me to sing to my father the verses I could recollect of our walking-song. I was sure the melody would cheer him, maybe even contribute to his recovery. I hummed the tune as I walked, summoning the lyrics in snatches from the depths of submerged memories. Anticipating my father's reaction, I smiled at the thought of his taking my hand and trying to sing along, or at least mouthing the words. When I arrived, however, the nurse in charge of the ward informed me that my father had died not long after I left him the previous afternoon. They had wanted to contact me, she said, but no one knew how to reach me. She assured me that he passed peacefully, in his sleep. It was as if he'd waited to see me one last time, and, having done so, could finally take flight from a world that had provoked in him such oppositions of gaiety and gloom.

I have thought much about my father since that day, and more and more I remark his influence on my life and character. Each of us was in his way one of life's problem children. Given the irregularities of our relationship, I suppose I was more immediately influenced by my mother's side of the family, but my father's spirit moves powerfully within me. From him I inherited a meditative mood and a taste for nature's solitudes. From my mother's line, which includes several lay intellectuals, and even one university professor, I inherited an appreciation for precision and a drive for knowledge. From my father, form; from my mother, content. Thus the tension within my spirit between artistry and scholarship.

Beside this tension there is in me another psychic strain, an inheritance from both sides of the family, if more directly from my father's line: a current of existential morbidity running through my life, flowing in turns beneath the surface, where though unseen it works its black magic nonetheless, and above ground whirling in circulating eddies of self-reflective despondency. *Acedia*, a painful sadness with the world, even unto the working of death, according to Christian teaching. *Taedium vitae*, a boredom with life, as learned Latinists have sometimes called it. *Melancholia*, according to the Greeks, an excess of black (*melaina*) bile (*cholê*), which Aristotle in his *Problemata* compares to the effects of drunkenness.

Aristotle's account of melancholia is curious, to say the least. In it one encounters definite points of contact with our contemporary understanding of the affliction, but also bizarre divergences. Those with an excess of black bile tend toward intellectual or artistic genius, he says, and he names Plato and Socrates as examples of the type, also "most of those concerned with poetry." This resonates with our idea of the saturnine artist and pondering man. But he adds that this effect depends on the bile's being overheated, which condition may also induce madness, lustfulness, or talkativeness, and these symptoms seem only distantly related to melancholy, if at all. As for those whose black bile is chilled, Aristotle says that they may be subject to unreasonable despondency and the inclination to suicide, which sounds very much like melancholy, shading into depression, as we experience these disorders; but he insists that these same people tend to be slow and stupid, which does not ring true at all. So whereas in our conception of melancholia we tend to associate creative genius with despondency, Aristotle separates them; and with each he associates other symptoms (loquacity and stupidity, for example) that have no place in our conception.

We are told that Aristotle's student Theophrastus composed a treatise *On Melancholy*, but nothing of any such work survives. Nor is there a description of the melancholy man in Theophrastus's extant *Characters*, a collection in which he sketches the personality traits of thirty different types of man. A puzzling omission if there were in fact, as Aristotle reports, such a number of melancholiacs among the great thinkers and artists of his day.

I have often wondered at the ancients' apparent lack of interest in melancholia. Is it not as lamentable as remarkable that Plato, for example, who wrote so eloquently, and so extensively, about goodness and virtue has left us not a single recommendation for preventing or curing the malaise of melancholia? And you will search in vain the tens of thousands of words which Aristotle wrote specifically on virtue and happiness for a mention of melancholia, much less for a prescription against it. And as for Epicurus, that philosophical physician of spiritual health *par excellence*, the mental disturbance from which he seeks relief is not our melancholia, however much in general terms his fear of the gods and fear of death may seem to resemble it. Read the man's letters: whatever condition he means to diagnose, it is not melancholia.

Since I myself am intimately acquainted with the symptoms of melancholia, through both personal experience and observation of my father, I record here an account of the melancholy man extracted from my notebooks which I composed some time ago in the spirit of Theophrastus's *Characters*:

Melancholia we may describe in brief as a state of wistful mournfulness regarding the whole of one's existence, to include the joyful as well as the sorrowful moments of one's life.

The melancholy man is periodically despondent and blue. He suffers from a sort of low-grade nostalgia for nothing in particular. He feels he has been deprived of something, but he can identify no specific item as the object of his concern. For example, he may regret the roads he didn't take while knowing full well that his way was best for him. He may mourn his lost youth even though he would not if given the chance relive it. He may grieve past lovers while sincerely insisting that he has no desire to rekindle the flame. In short, the return (nostos) for which he aches (algos) lacks specific content, and therefore he suspects that in the deepest sense his problem is not a frustrated longing for home, but rather that he has no home to revisit, and never has. He is adrift in a void seeking solid ground. In the end perhaps he'd like to return to the warm blankness of the womb, or to crawl back into non-being.

Nor is the melancholy man exclusively nostalgic. He suffers also from anticipatory grief. Conjuring before his mind's eye future pains and sorrow, he suffers from them in the present. Even his future happiness grieves him, for he envisions also its passing.

But no man can fully represent the type who does not also treasure his pain, even to the extent of seeking it out. His ache is a foretaste of death, and although the melancholy man is not necessarily suicidal, he is comforted by anticipations of the end. A strange sort of comfort, to be sure, the comfort of a sick child abed in the care of his mother. Fuzzy head and warm blankets; half asleep throughout the day; staying home from school. For the melancholy man, life itself is at times the sickness, old age the warmth, and death his tender mother. The final ministrations.

The melancholy man is not bitter, gruff, or rude. He may be perfectly polite, amiable and affable. His condition rather lies beneath his general public affect. If it surfaces in company, it may appear as a distracted lack of interest in contemporary concerns, a smile that masks no ill-will but which seems somehow forced.

And to conclude with a poetic flourish, we may say that of the seasons the melancholy man resembles late autumn: yellow leaves wind-tossed on an ocher field, early snow on the crests of neighboring hills. As weather he is an overcast afternoon: low-hanging clouds; no rain, but no sun. He is the scent on the breeze of honey-suckle or freshly mown hay, the wrenching of sensual memories. He is a faded photograph of his father as a child.

In short, the melancholy man regards the life of an individual, like the history of the West, as a steady decline from romantic mystery to prosaic disenchantment. His world wears out its wonder.

Thus my attempt at a Theophrastan account of melancholia. It is only a sketch, I know, but in this I adhere to the example of the *Characters*. I'm afraid I haven't the time or energy, nor the wickedly diverse learning, of a Robert Burton.

But to return to my father, my recollections of whose life and death have prompted these reflections: I recall that my father used to say, "The good I can usually manage. It's joy that eludes me." This self-assessment may not have been altogether accurate, for the man on occasion indisputably fell short of the good, especially later in life. But I take his point, particularly since his lapses in virtue were in some sense voluntary. I mean to say that my father's vices were not the issue of ignorance, psychic injustice, or weakness of will (as Socrates, Plato, and Aristotle would have it), but rather they resulted from a sort of willed perversity, an intentional assault on the pretty seductions of conventional ethical standards. Not to suggest that my father doubted the objectivity of these standards. I'm sure he never gave the matter the depth of thought required to come to this conclusion. Rather I suspect he subverted the good while faithfully accepting it as good, that he knowingly acted against his own interests in a frustration of self-laceration, as a chained animal will gnaw its own tail or maul its hide.

And even if my father's bad habits were involuntary, still I think the ancient ethicists fail to account for his failures of character. He suffered from an existential displacement, as I have explained, and even though he was not to blame for the fact—neither for that matter was his father, the floods, the cosmos, God, or the absence of God—despite the "innocence" of his being thus out of time, out of his proper atmosphere, and consequently out of sorts psychologically, nevertheless he punished himself as if he were guilty. Hence his occasional indulgence in vice. But whenever his life was going well, he was as virtuous as any mild-mannered little Nicomachus.

I stress my father's capacity for virtue to recall my earlier expression of wonder at the ancients' fixation on ethics to the near total neglect of melancholia. For it seems to me that a well-reared individual will with age and experience sort out virtue and vice for himself. He may well require the assistance and encouragement of his family, his peers, and the appropriate enculturation, including explicit education in the theory and practice of virtue (though this last is far from necessary). But this is just to say that the human animal must *learn* to become fully human, that our untutored nature will not do the work for us, as it operates among the other animals. When young, one may in minor matters indulge in every variety of venial vice; but unless one is corrupt at core, eventually one will find one's way to virtue. This state is called "maturity."

But if virtue is so readily acquired, why were the ancient philosophers so preoccupied with the subject? Why the continual production of theories, arguments, allegories, and exhortations, the speeches, songs, letters, poems, treatises, and books? And why the relative paucity of attention to our psychological, spiritual, and existential condition? Were the men of their time so much more inclined to vice than we are today? Were they less disposed to melancholy? I cannot bring myself to believe it.

Perhaps we should regard the Greeks' obsession with virtue as at least in part an acknowledgement of the presence of melancholia among them. Maybe virtue was their prescription for a cure. Given the social-political strife that often thrust the city-states into frenzies of murderous civil war, with a hostility among factions simmering even in times of peace, it may well be that virtue and vice, in and for themselves, were necessary subjects for public reflection. It may also be that the Hellenistic ethicists' concern with *hêdonê*, *ataraxia*, and *apatheia*—with, that is to say, pleasure, freedom from mental disturbance, and mastery of one's passions and emotions—make explicit themes that were implicit in the work of their Classical predecessors.

The so-called "Wisdom of Silenus" goes back through the Classical period (it appeared for example in a lost work of Aristotle) into the Archaic. Theognis recounts it in a poem as if it were ancient in his day. According to the story,

Silenus the satyr, having been captured by king Midas, in return for his freedom revealed that the best of all things for mortals is never to have been born, and second best to die as soon as possible. This certainly expresses a gloomy view of human existence, and one may well project a strain of melancholia into the hearts and minds of the people among whom this perspective thrived.

But what a peculiar phenomenon is melancholia! One marvels that men are so often so very unhappy. So tense, anxious, and fearful, so full of sorrow and self-doubt. It's as though we sense that something fundamental is unbalanced at our core. A something unspecifiable and unnamable. And I suspect it's worse that the malady is not lethal, but rather troubling, unsettling, dispiriting, like a pinprick of disquiet whose source one cannot identify, and which never goes away.

Once at a gathering of my extended family I overheard a young cousin announce that "Life is fun!" in the midst of his childish play. I often wonder what he would say today, twenty years on, and what he will say if he reflects on the matter twenty years from now. As playtime has long since come to an end, and real life commenced, I doubt that "fun" will spring immediately to mind. At best one might expect "confusing," "absurd," or "difficult," but more likely will be "disappointing" or "vexatious." Life is suffering, the Buddha said, and for two thousand years men have conceded the point, even insisted on it. But what if one wishes to overcome suffering not by exchanging desire for an arid asceticism, but by transcending it into cheerfulness? Where is the physician who knows the prescription for this therapy of joy?

"Joy eludes me," my father said, and I suppose this sums up one aspect of the human condition. Even the ancients' *eudaimonia*, the good life of virtue, does not ensure happiness as cheerfulness, as the absence of melancholia. Nor I think does a virtuous life render these states more likely than not, not much more likely anyway. In short, though virtue may be necessary for a good life, it is not sufficient. Whence then comes my father's elusive joy? One would appreciate the insight of the truly great minds on this matter, just one short dialogue from Plato's hand, the scraps of Aristotle's lecture notes. Alas, we have nothing.

Our ignorance on this point is particularly disturbing because the thinking man who cannot overcome his melancholy is prone to slip into a still graver condition. I recall conversations with my friend on the subject of nihilism, a theme which when I first made his acquaintance he had recently determined to think through to its end. Over the years he explored a number of different accounts of the origin and nature of the condition, all of them as insightful as provocative. Here I set down the terms as I recall them of one particular formulation that resonates at this moment of sustained reflection on my relationship with my father.

In the West we have believed in and expected, at times even actively sought, an end-state of cosmic history, a *telos* to supply a meaning and purpose to the whole and to each of its parts. This end might have been the arrival of the Kingdom of God, a fully realized moral world order, peace

and harmony among the nations, or even universal annihilation, which if unpleasant would at least mark the
fulfillment of a goal. But today we no longer believe in final
causes: neither the universe, world history, nor an
individual human life progresses with an innate direction-
ality. Nothing "progresses." Events occur; happenings just
happen.

We have also believed in an organizing-unifying structure
that undergirds and envelops all things, as if each individual
were a node within a grand unity, every man occupying his
proper place in the whole, like a piece fit snug in a well-
designed puzzle. We have imagined ourselves as creatures of
God assigned to a particular time and place specifically to
contribute to the best of all possible worlds; or as rational
expressions of the rational unfolding of the universal rational
Spirit, each individual a sensible component of a sensible
whole. But today we no longer believe in the Whole as
anything beyond our own imaginative construct. Thus we
are no longer comforted by the thought that we exist when,
where, and as we are meant to. We ourselves and our
surroundings are not modeled on a scheme designed by a
beneficent and rational Demiurge. We just are. Then one
day we are not.

We have believed moreover in the Truth of Being
manifesting as a True World, the really Real, whether as
Plato's realm of Forms, Plotinus's One, the Christians'
God, Kant's noumenon, Schopenhauer's Will, or the
scientists' facts and truths. But today at last we understand
that we ourselves have fabricated this True World, raised it
from the depths of our need for comforting illusions against

the absence of meaning, purpose, unity, and truth in *this* world. But since for so long now we have dismissed this world as merely apparent, we suffer from the thought that we too in the end may be mere appearances, shadows flitting through a dream with no fundament of the "real" at our core, nor any external "real" to which we might find our way through reasoning or prayer while alive, or as reward for intellectual or moral virtue after death.

Moreover, and finally, our *belief in the value of existence* has from time immemorial been bound up with these convictions regarding our teleological orientation, our place within a harmonious whole, and our relationship to truth. Even more than bound up with: logically dependent on. We have believed that life has value precisely *because* it is related to a goal, to a unity, and to the truth. Therefore those who lose their faith in final goals, unity, and truth—in short, the metaphysical nihilists—tend to succumb to the conviction that *life is meaningless, pointless, and valueless*, which conviction we may call psychological nihilism.

Looking back on my father's life, I have determined that he likely suffered from psychological nihilism. Not to suggest he'd reasoned his way through the conditions as I have outlined them to arrive at nihilism as their conclusion. As deep as he was in his way, he was not a thinking man. His spirit was rather an abyss of the unconscious profundities of nature, excavated by feeling rather than by thought. He was, let us say, an intuitive nihilist. He had *lived* the stages on the way to nihilism; he had no need to *think* them too.

And as for myself: I too was in danger of losing myself so thoroughly in the haze of melancholia as to draw the nihilistic conclusion, or rather to *be* this drawn conclusion, to live the anti-life of this terrible inference. For as I have noted already in other contexts, however salutary the intellectual changes I'd begun to effect under the care of my friend in the mountains, I still had found no way to incorporate them into my life in the urban lowlands.

V

The Wanderer and His Shadow

My dear Charmides,

I received your letter, my friend, this very afternoon, and I thank you for it. Despite my love of—my *need* for—solitude, I value friendship dearly. In this regard at least I remain an Epicurean.

I still linger here around our favorite lakes and meadows, so your post arrived in my hands directly, no aberrating diversions required. The atmosphere is as brilliant as when you were present, the mountains and sky every bit as sublime—more, even, if this is possible, for elemental nature today reposes as if touched by the melancholy foreboding of autumn, which infuses every color, sound, and scent with an additional note of soulfulness. I will be leaving soon, seasoned old wanderer that I am, though I have not yet made precise arrangements. Therefore please do forward your reply to my associate in Basel, as we discussed before you left. He will know where to find me (likely even before I do, which is his way, or rather mine—Ha!), and he will make sure your letters reach me until I send you a new address.

How sorry I am to learn of your father's passing. I know you had hoped to avoid the event while in your present state. And to have lost him on the very day of your first visit in years—really, how uncanny! I lost my own father when I was a child of five, so I knew him only as a child knows the world, which is to say but slightly, from one narrow angle, as it were. But also innocently, merrily. There are uses as well as disadvantages to this, as I'm sure you can imagine. I lacked a properly masculine upbringing, which made me too bookish a sort, and insufficiently active. For years I have feared that I too would die young, and even though I have now outlived the man, I expect it yet. At times I feel that my father inhabits me as a sort of sickness, a specter of death suffusing me which strains against my living self. It weakens me. Despite this physiological handicap, however, the early loss made me from my youth a thoughtful, serious soul, which I reckon on balance a good thing. Let us call it a spiritual benefit, and not a minor one at that.

You have lost your father as a mature adult bereaved of an older man, which under normal conditions would be most natural and appropriate. But as I understand the circumstances of your estrangement, the facts of your fractured relationship have likely exercised eccentric influences upon your person. And in this case too there doubtless are advantages and disadvantages. I will not presume to speculate as to their nature, but I urge you to identify and cultivate the virtues that have sprouted in you even from this tainted soil. And as for the so-called vices, turn these too to your advantage; prune them, tame them, nurture them in such a way as to bend them to your benefit. For even very suffering may be good for the man possessed of the will and spiritual strength to metabolize and absorb the pain as fuel, energy, and power-potential.

But perhaps this is a matter best addressed in person. It is good when walking through the gloom to proceed arm in arm with a friend. Therefore I leave off until we meet again, which I do hope will be soon.

You have asked that I restate and elaborate the thoughts I shared with you on the value of truth during our peripatetic conversations in the days before you left. Of course I am happy to do so, though perhaps I shall refrain from treating every detail in a single letter. Permit me to propose instead that we pursue this theme through an epistolic exchange. In this way we shall simulate the dialectic of conversation, which I expect will contribute to concision and clarity, and thereby to mutual comprehension. In this way, moreover, we shall prolong our interaction, and, as I am sure you will agree, it is always good to savor the good.

To begin with, then, I should stress that in the following remarks I intend by "truth" to refer to the way the world, or reality, or Being, really is, in and of and for itself, as they say, independent of any *a priori* human contribution, unmediated and therefore unmodified by our physical-psychic organization, or, if you prefer, the particular innate structure of our sensory-cognitive apparatus—in the Kantian or Schopenhauerian sense, you understand. I refer, in short, to reality independent of biologically conditioned interpretations of the "text" of the world. The truth, then, is supposed to represent this text as it is, free of every tendentious interpretation, the reality behind the appearances, the noumenon behind the phenomena. (Supposed by some, that is—not by me.)

So, now, as to knowledge of the truth:

Maybe there is no truth.

Maybe there is truth, but it is unknowable. Wholly unknowable, or knowable only in scattered parts.

Maybe there is truth, and it is wholly knowable, but we can never know that we know it.

Maybe there is truth, and it is altogether wholly knowable, but to know it is bad, dangerous, harmful, or deadly.

Maybe there is truth, and it is knowable and good to know, but to know it is no better than not to know it.

Maybe there is truth, and it is knowable, and it is better to know than not to know it, but other things are better still: depth, creativity, beauty, vitality, foolishness, free-spiritedness.

Maybe there is truth, and it is knowable, and to know it is best of all, but not directly seeking it is the best way to find it, or seeking it directly is only one among several suitable methods.

Maybe there is truth, and it is knowable, and to know it is best of all, and to seek it is the best way to find it, but there is no urgency to know it now. Perhaps the truth withdraws from overzealous, hurried and harried suitors.

What do we know of truth in advance to eliminate any of these possibilities?

With these remarks I have not descended into the depths of the matter at hand, I know. I haven't meant to. I intend only to relax your convictions, or to encourage you to relax yourself in relation to them. To disengage from your fixated will to truth, if only somewhat and if only temporarily, for the sake of intellectual experimentation and creative exploration. Later, if you like, you may return to your pursuit of knowledge of the truth. Nothing prevents you, after all, and you still have years to live.

I will, however, close with the following more intentionally provocative suggestions:

Even granting, *arguendo*, that truth exists, perhaps it is but the flowering of untruth. For the idea that a noumenal realm of things-in-themselves lurks behind the phenomenal appearances is itself an intellectual artifact of the phenomenal realm, and therefore likely to be itself merely apparently true, which is to say *false*. And here we return to the human contribution I mentioned above. Say that there is truth: then truth might well exist only because we ourselves have created it. Say that we may yet discover the truth: then truth might be a treasure that we ourselves have buried. For perhaps we encounter in the world only that which we ourselves have set down into it.

Supposing, then, that we want truth. Fine. But *why not rather untruth*?

I say that as philosophers we should aim to transcend our petty beliefs and unbeliefs, and even our so-called "knowledge." For our aim is not knowledge of the truth. Our aim is wisdom.

Old Solon was wise, was he not? But what did he know of truth?

Perhaps I shall conclude with this. It will do as a preamble to our exchange, no? I await your reply, with all good will, I assure you. I add only this final thought: *eu prattein*, my friend, as our old Plato would say. Be well and do well.

Your Friend in the mountains

21 August

My Friend,

What a delight it was to receive and read your letter! I felt almost as if we were together again, this feeling enhanced by your evocation of the beauty of our mountain valley. How I hated to leave, but of course it couldn't be helped. I certainly hope to return next summer, and to see and speak with you again there too.

I buried my father the day before I received your letter. I do appreciate your kind words. Thank you. How sad it is to witness the interment of a man with no one but oneself moved to mourn him. And what was the point of the life, then? He performed various actions, affected this person or that in minor ways. He begat me. But to what end? A man departs, dies, and the elements rush in to fill the void, like the sea overrunning a footprint in the sand: when the water streams out the beach is brushed smooth, as if no mark had ever been imprinted there. A vacuum to commemorate the absence, a small breach in the universe, as it were, would be bleak but at least a monument of sorts, a reminder of former presence. Instead, it's as if one never existed.

Ah, time passes and all is forgotten. Everyone and everything. To no end, to no end.

But, as you say, perhaps it is best to discuss grim matters in company with another. To contemplate the heavens' groan while sitting alone in the dark tends to magnify one's sense of isolation...

So, then: to address your questions and observations regarding truth, knowledge, and wisdom. I must say I find it hard to engage the suggestion that there is no truth. For does not the proposition "There is no truth" amount to the claim that "It is true that there is no truth"? Is not a proposition an assertion, the assertion of the truth of the content of the proposition? And if this is so, as I believe it is, then the proposition "There is no truth" is self-contradictory. And as we know from Aristotle, it makes no sense whatever to violate or deny the Law of Non-Contradiction. For to deny it is to assert that it is false, false as opposed to true. But the distinction between the false and the true depends on this very law. One thereby affirms it in the very act of attempting to deny it, which is to say, quite literally, that it is impossible actually to deny the law. The critic's apparent denial is but verbal legerdemain.

But it may be that I misunderstand you on this point. Despite my academic specialization, logical thickets do sometimes entangle and prick me. Therefore I pass on to other matters. And to appeal again to Aristotle, and specifically to the first book of his *Metaphysics*, I note that he presents therein an admirable case for identifying wisdom with a certain kind of knowledge.

The man who knows a skill or craft (a *technê*)—the carpenter or the general, for example—is thought to be more admirable than the man skilled merely from experience. Both men may engage successfully in the relevant activity, but the man who possesses knowledge of the causes involved appears to us wiser than the merely experienced man. The man who knows understands the *why* of his actions, the causes and principles that render them successful, and moreover he thereby possesses universal knowledge within the relevant domain. He can apply his craft in novel circumstances beyond those of which he has had direct experience. The merely experienced man as it were feels his way through, and he knows only that *this* particular act was successful on *this* particular occasion. He cannot with confidence universalize his knowledge to different but relevantly similar cases. Moreover, the man who knows, and especially the man who knows the causes to the highest degree, who possesses an account or theory (a *logos*) of the activity, is considered wise to a higher degree, in particular because he can teach the craft to others.

Men first began to philosophize from wonder, Aristotle says, and the earliest philosophers were motivated by the drive to dispel ignorance rather than the need to accomplish anything in particular. Moreover, all men regard wisdom as the science of the first causes and principles, and this science is theoretical rather than productive, which is to say it results in understanding rather than in practical activity.

Furthermore, the science of the first causes and principles is explanatory of the subordinate sciences, whose causes and principles operate in dependence on its own. It accounts for the ends of all activities, and thereby knows the good in each case. It is the most independent and self-sufficient of the sciences, for it is not subject to any superior or directorial end. And it is, as we have seen, the most teachable, for to teach is to explain the causes of things.

Finally, this science is also the most divine of all the sciences, for God is agreed by everyone to be among the first causes and principles, and in fact to be the highest of them all. According to this account, then, wisdom is knowledge of the divine. And since God is also Truth, wisdom must be knowledge of the truth.

This last point is confirmed by Aristotle's discussion of wisdom in the *Ethics*. In the sixth book of that work we learn that the rational part of the soul may be divided into the so-called rationally-calculating inferior part, and the superior part, which Aristotle calls contemplative or scientific. The virtue of the rationally-calculating part of the soul is prudence or practical wisdom (*phronêsis*), which is knowledge of changeable things, contingent beings, and is therefore applicable to mundane practical actions and activities. The virtue of the contemplative or scientific part is theoretical wisdom or, simply, wisdom (*sophia*), which is knowledge of unchanging, everlasting, and necessary beings or principles. Wisdom in turn is composed of two constituent elements, certain or scientific knowledge (*epistêmê*), which is knowledge of the conclusion of an inductive or deductive demonstration, and intuitive understanding (*nous*), which is knowledge of the truth of the indemonstrable principles of a demonstration. Since this contemplative or scientific part of the soul is the altogether highest element of man, its virtue, wisdom, is the greatest good for man. And, as we have seen, wisdom is manifest in and through knowledge.

One last thing, this time touching on Plato. Does not Plato too equate wisdom with knowledge of the truth? In his *Symposium* for instance, when Diotima insists that the gods neither philosophize nor desire to become wise, she refers to her earlier remarks on knowledge and ignorance, in which place she speaks of knowledge and wisdom (*epistêmê* and *sophia*) interchangeably. Her argument, in brief, is that the gods do not philosophize because they are already wise by virtue of their knowledge.

I suppose this is a good place to stop for now. I do apologize for the pedantic tone, but, well, Aristotle you know! Dry as he may be, however, I am persuaded by his argument. And I did at least spice up my dish with a dash of Plato for dessert. You'll thank me for that I trust.

A safe journey to you, my friend, if you relocate before I hear from you again. And, whenever you do depart, please give my best—with a wave or a nod of the head—to the meadows, mountains, and lakes. Oh, how I miss them!

I look forward to hearing from you as soon as you are settled and find it convenient to write. Until then, I wish you all the best.

Charmides (the Younger)

***

12 September

Charmides, my friend,

My Basel associate has successfully forwarded your letter to me here in my new residence. I received it just yesterday. I am presently in Genoa, where I have found a small but quiet and high-ceilinged room with a south-facing window which looks out on the sea. In many ways this is my ideal. I shall stay here through the winter. This is my intention, anyway, though my plans do tend to change with the weather (I mean this quite literally, by the way), so we shall see. In any case, you may reach me directly at the enclosed address until I indicate otherwise.

Now on to your "pedantic" letter. How I delighted in it! There is a certain charm to Aristotle, stuffy old professor that he was. I can't help but imagine him smiling as he composed his lectures, full of himself, no doubt, a touch too prideful, but also with a harmless sort of good will. Yet with this modest expression of admiration my esteem for the man exhausts itself. Aristotle's objectionable habit of regarding his own peculiar system as the *telos* of all prior philosophy, his insistent misreading of the Pre-Platonic philosophers as immature thinkers striving in vain to formulate ideas that he alone would adequately express—this is all too well known to belabor. Equally annoying is his tendency to reduce the colossus wisdom to the size of a bauble toted about in the book-bag of a smug schoolmarm, jostling against old bits of chalk and soiled tissues. Who but a pedagogue would dare equate wisdom with knowledge, and appeal to teachability as justification?!

The ancients tell us that Aristotle was a bookish man, his personal library rivalled only by Euripides' collection. Plato apparently called him the Reader. But you are familiar with the reports, I'm sure. Now what must we make of the cogitations of so prosaic a soul, a man inclined above all else to sit alone for hours with his head buried in a book? Let him keep his head down, I say, and his mouth shut.

But to be serious. (Not that I haven't been serious so far.) Aristotle claims that the man with knowledge of the craft is more admirable than the man with skill who lacks knowledge. But this is not necessarily so, is it? Consider the case in which the non-knower is the superior craftsman by instinct or muscle-memory (and here I think of what you have told me of your father's craftsmanship). Then we might even mock the man who knows. Of course it is true that if the knower and the non-knower are equally accomplished in their craft, we prefer the man who knows. But this does not prove that we judge knowledge to be of supreme worth without qualification. Rather it indicates only that in some situations we count knowledge an additional item of value.

Now compare the skilled knowing craftsman to the unknowing but inspired artist. In this case too we are likely to rank the non-knower higher. Do we not judge the mad poet superior to the knowledgeable stonemason? And according to Plato in the *Phaedrus* the mad poet is superior even to the sane poet who possesses the relevant *technê*, which is to say the poet who knows. In the *Ion* he goes even further, insisting that the accomplished poet operates altogether without his intellect (his *nous*), and that no man is able to produce either poetry or prophecy while in his right mind. If this is so, then we will not count knowledge an additional item of value—quite the opposite. Knowledge may well inhibit the expression of the poet's gifts, may utterly extinguish the flame of his inspired artistry. The artist, like the athlete, must act at times exclusively from instinct; even a moment's deliberation would mar his performance.

A Philosophical Fiction

Let us be honest now, and frank: Aristotle himself admired knowledge, as a teacher will, and therefore he selected and read his examples to confirm his biases. The Medievals called him The Philosopher. I call him *Il Maestro*, The Schoolmaster. Aristotle was the first professor of philosophy, and he valued knowledge in part because he valued teaching. Are not his voluminous lecture notes testimony to his intellectual orientation? I adjudge the man the pedant-rogue who diverted the *eros* of intellect away from original creative wisdom (as manifest for instance in Solon's poetry and legislation) and set it on the arid path to wisdom-as-science, or, in contemporary terms, *Wissenschaft*.

In his *Metaphysics* Aristotle writes of *sophia* on the model of know-how, which as you know was one accepted sense of the word among the ancients, a sense which appears at times even in Plato's dialogues. But this is the pedestrian meaning of the word, as employed by and about actual craftsmen, blacksmiths and medical doctors for example. Is this the sense of "wisdom" for which we are on the hunt? No, surely this is not the object of *our* love, we who are not pedestrian craftsmen but rather philosophers, we *mad, mad lovers of wisdom!!*

Now, on the matter of truth and contradiction, I shall be brief. To address the problem thoroughly—which is to say, to the satisfaction of your typical university philoso-phaster—would require a lengthy dissertation, and I am constitutionally predisposed against loquacity. Therefore the following shall have to suffice.

Do the venerated axioms of logic adequately represent the nature of reality, of Being? Do they disclose the essence of truth? To know this, to know rather than presume, we should have to possess knowledge of reality and truth independent of the axioms. But this we do not have. Consequently we do not know. All that we can say with confidence is that these so-called "laws of thought" (ah, just think of the variety of assumptions smuggled into this use of the word *law*!) seem to mirror the patterns of our thinking. But to say that "We cannot affirm and deny one and the same thing" is to acknowledge an incapacity; it does not pick out a mark of reality or truth independent of the human constitution. Perhaps we learn here something about our biology or psychology, but we learn nothing about the truth. Alternatively, if we cannot declare with confidence that "One and the same thing cannot be both true and false," and we are not content to take these "laws" of thought for bare indications of the limitations of our intellect, then we are left with the *imperative*, "Do not both affirm and deny one and the same thing." But *with this we are on moral ground*, and we have abandoned any pretense to the objective pursuit of the truth of Being.

Finally, on this topic: When I am in a high-spirited mood, I am often inclined to think—or even, when walking enraptured alone among the wildflowers, to shout to the winds,

Nothing is true! Everything is permitted!

Is this self-contradictory? But we needn't take this as an assertoric proposition, as they say, as a truth-claim. No. It is rather an expression of intellectual exuberance, a declaration of philosophical liberation. And in this sense I regard it even as *weightier* than any measured attempt to assert the truth.

But enough with old Aristotle. Let us leave him to his lectern. I have additional thoughts to share regarding Plato—another poet and legislator, by the way, in the tradition of his ancestor Solon—specifically regarding his conception of wisdom, to which you refer in connection with the *Symposium*. But perhaps it is best to defer this until later in our exchange, for now I would like to address, if only briefly, your remarks concerning death and existential meaning, or the lack thereof.

Your lament is as old as Solomon, as of course you understand. But despite the hoary age, the Preacher's insight remains sound. The labors of a human life are indeed vexation of spirit and a chasing after wind. All is vanity, and in the end it comes to nothing, ourselves included. Will it ease your pain if I remark that the hard kernel of existence incites us nutcrackers of the spirit to the action we most delight in? Yet, sad to say, this redemptive insight has eluded us since that malicious old Athenian wizard insisted that reason can correct being and heal the eternal wound of existence. But Socrates was naive, and his optimism was a symptom of a fundamentally nihilistic drive. He said No! to life at every turn, whereas we who strive to be Yes-sayers affirm even our suffering.

If life has no inherent meaning or purpose, then we must meet the challenge—or perhaps I should call it a gift of freedom—to provide it with a meaning ourselves by plowing our *will* into it. Thus do we become creators, self-creators, the artists of our own destiny. And where would the value in this be if life were intrinsically saturated with happiness, pleasure, and plump bourgeois contentment? No, I say: Let hardship serve as a stimulant to the creative act, for *creation redeems suffering*. Is this not the lesson of Greek tragedy? And had not the Greeks attained their maximum in and through their tragic age, before the buffoons of reason mystified them with their silly obsessions with virtue and happiness? Let us learn then from the tragic Greeks, from Aeschylus for example, who spilled blood on the field at Marathon and sang the *Oresteia*.

But, well, now I have written more on this matter than I intended to. I've elaborated your personal pain to nearly universal dimensions. Do forgive me. Yet I hope that on reflection you will agree that my remarks on suffering and creativity are not irrelevant to my analysis of knowledge and wisdom. For he who overcomes his lust for knowledge of truth may through this self-surmounting realize that all is permitted to the philosopher who expresses his love of wisdom in the exuberance of inspired creation.

But I suppose that we should discuss this further on another occasion. Therefore I shall now leave off and await your reply. I lay down my pen to step outside for a stroll along the quay, for the warm salt air beckons to me through my window.

My best to you, dear Charmides, and, please, do let me know about your health.

Your friend

Ah, friend Charmides,

Here I sit writing to you on the very evening of the day I posted my previous letter. I had promised to defer my remarks about Plato until a later date, but as I walked along the harbor in the afternoon, reflecting on the letter I had just sent off to you, the heaving sea spoke to me insistently of Plato, the most confounding enigma among the ancient philosophers, including even the riddling Heraclitus. Therefore I could not help myself. Therefore this second letter of the day.

Recall the volume of Plato I carried when we met. I was then rereading the *Phaedo*. I am studying it still, or rather exploring it, I should say, for it is a labyrinth. In my past as a pedagogue I used to read the *Phaedo* with my students of Greek—to teach them the language, of course, but my deeper motive was to infect them with philosophy! A labyrinth, I called the work, and a labyrinth it is. Its winding walls are composed of layers of Platonism, and Socrates as the mouthpiece of Platonic doctrine is the Minotaur at the center of the structure. He is killed in the end, as he must be, as he *should* be, and we readers are permitted to witness his death after passing through the maze. Thereby are we liberated, saved as were those "twice seven" youths whom Theseus led to Crete and saved from death, and "was saved himself." Socrates thinks the liberation will be his, that finally he will be released from the cycle of rebirth to live forever as a pure soul eternally free from the bonds of the body. But of course he is mistaken, and his *logos* of the immortal soul is but the mask of a *mythos*. It is from this that we are liberated: There is no such soul, and consequently no release from life. But who is it saves us from this illusion, and in so doing is saved himself? Who else but Plato? Through the *Phaedo* Plato saves us from Socratic Platonism, and he saves himself as architect of the Minotaur's labyrinth, as the creative force behind Platonic dogma, behind but independent of it, more capacious than Platonism, master of it, superior, supreme. I like to think that Plato executed Socrates to prevent us philosophers of the future from being devoured by this Minotaur of reason. Plato with his stylus in hand, Plato the thinker-artist, Plato the sage for whom the Platonic philosopher was but a monstrous and frightening mask.

When meditating on the mystery of Plato I make a point to distinguish his characters' words as spoken in the dialogues from his own intentions as author of the works. We must not rashly identify what *they say* with what *he* aims to *do*. Consider that the first word of the *Phaedo*, *autos*, stresses the question Echecrates puts to Phaedo whether *he himself* was present on the day that Socrates died. And with the first word of his reply, *autos*, Phaedo insists that, yes, *I myself* was there. From their initial exchange, then, the characters establish, to their own satisfaction, the reliability of Phaedo's account. But then Phaedo reports that Plato was not present. And what does *this* establish? For the characters in the dialogue, this is merely one more fact among others, information of no particular consequence. But the thoughtful reader will recognize the dramatic irony. We know more than the characters know; our knowledge encompasses theirs and extends beyond it. In this particular instance, we know that Plato is the author of Phaedo's words. Therefore we must also know that if Plato was not present for the events his character Phaedo recounts, we cannot trust Phaedo's words. In short, then, Plato's absence establishes for the thoughtful reader a doubt concerning the reliability of Phaedo's account, which is to say of the *Phaedo* itself as composed by Plato as an ostensibly historical document.

Moreover and more specifically, when Echecrates inquires whether anyone was present to witness the things that Socrates said and did at the moment of *auton ton thanaton*, the *death itself*, Plato specifically calls into question his version of Socrates' final moments, including of course the dying man's famous last words. Could it be that Socrates never asked his friend to sacrifice a rooster to Asklepios? Could the request be Plato's creative invention? And if so, to what end did he conjure this? Did he intend his readers to question the fitness of Socrates' spirit?

Forgive me: I go into these details to urge the following point. Though it may well be that the characters in Plato's dialogues value and seek the truth, and identify wisdom with knowledge, nevertheless we cannot assume that Plato himself shares their perspective. We know very little of Plato as an individual, of course, but we do know this for certain: he conceived and composed the dialogues. And from this we may infer other remarkable specifics. Unlike Socrates, Plato was a writer. Socrates passed his time in public, often in the city center, talking with his fellow citizens. Plato resided in a grove outside the city walls, and he spent much of his time in solitude, writing, or thinking about his writing. Consider the Platonic corpus, its breadth and extent, and consequently the hours, days, months, years that Plato dedicated not only to writing but to formulating the dialogues, to plotting and planning, combing and curling, editing and revising them, to dreaming up new themes and settings, new metaphors, images, arguments, myths, and so on.

Now ask yourself what Plato did from day to day. I can't help but picture the man alone, strolling through the grove of *Hekadêmos*, absorbing the colors, sounds, and scents of primal nature fecund and undisturbed, nourishing his creative intellect by walking and reflecting, pondering, fantasizing, thinking about the work he was then composing. My point, then, is this: Plato was more than an intellectual; he was also a poet. Therefore I have called him a "thinker-artist."

Since Plato wrote the dialogues *as a philosopher*, his writing—the very fact as well as the style of his writing—must illuminate his conception of the proper activity of the lover of wisdom, and thereby also his conception of wisdom itself. Now, do the dialogues read to you like documents through which Plato means to state the truth directly and unambiguously? Are they ordered collections of justified claims to knowledge, as Aristotle's works are evidently meant to be? Of course not. Not at all.

At this point certain fastidious scholars will appeal to Socrates' critique of writing in the *Phaedrus* to object to my taking the dialogues seriously as expressions of philosophy.

The dialogues are mere play, they will insist, not philosophy in themselves but reminders of philosophy for those who know. Philosophy manifests exclusively in speech, face to face, through rigorous dialectic. But here I must dissent, for on this particular, as on so many, I cannot take Socrates seriously. And why should I? Plato undermines the old man's staid pronouncements from the opening scene of the *Phaedrus*, for the beauty of the trees beyond the city walls taught Plato more than Socrates learned from engaging in debate with urban sophisticates. No, I do not trust him. Really, can you imagine Plato expending such energy over fifty years toward the end of producing *mere* play? I cannot. The dialogues may well be play, but they are *serious* play, as is all deep art, as is all wisdom. For what is wisdom but an artistry of the depths, a playful seriousness, the profundity of the heights and a thoughtful foolishness?

I need not repeat the ancient stories of Plato's composing tragedies in his youth. Nor of his erecting a shrine to the Muses on the grounds of the Academy, the Muses to whom in the *Phaedrus* we learn the cicadas sing the praises of those who live a philosophical life, which is itself a way of honoring the Muses' arts. You know all this well, I am sure. But perhaps you have not yet grasped the relevant implications. Plato was no proto-scholar or scientist, no *wissenschaftlicher Mensch*, as the Germans say. How strangely we forget that Plato was neither Socrates nor Aristotle! Plato was an altogether different type, eccentric and untimely—he was a philosopher-artist. The love of beauty suffused his love of wisdom because his wisdom was a mad creative overflowing; it resembled the act of an amoral artist-god who delights in creation and destruction, in discharging the pressure of the pregnant oppositions swelling and revolving in his soul—truth and falsity, fact and fiction, consistency and contradiction, gravity and gaiety, history and prophecy, scientific investigation and poetry. These oppositions intermingled and interfused are generative of art as offspring, art not only as dialogue but art as mind, as spirit, as *life*.

As I have said, Plato was a poet and a legislator: he imagined and decreed new thought-worlds and novel modes of inhabiting them. Thus did he express his love of wisdom.

But forgive me, friend Charmides, for burdening you with so long an addendum to my previous letter. As I say, I could not help myself. Plato and the sea provoked me to it. Please do take your time replying. I understand the strains of your other pressing concerns and responsibilities. I am not yet so detached from the workaday world as to imagine every man as idle as myself. Having said this, however, I do look forward to reviewing your reaction to my thoughts, which must seem at times the ravings of a madman. To other men, anyway. As for myself, I love my wicked thoughts as my own most beautiful offspring and companions!

And so finally now to conclude, which I do as I closed my previous letter: Please do let me know how you are, and, as always, my very best to you.

Your Friend

15 October

Dear friend,

Please accept my apologies for having taken so long to reply to your stimulating pair of letters. I have been unwell. My father's death affected me more profoundly than I had realized. The black bile roiled in me and swelled to such a turbulent depth it overthrew the balance of my humors. Oh, melancholia! For days I drifted in darkness, my head and heart a static of gloomy confusion. But as the academic year was fast approaching, I tried despite my condition to prepare my lectures and to continue work on my present research projects. This was anything but prudent! I suffered an attack in the head of such proportions as I have never before experienced. I lay supine in a lifeless swoon for a week. Pain was less the problem than an unrelenting state of oneiric semi-consciousness. At times I felt as if my body had collapsed into a paralysis of hibernation. Yet my mind was wildly active, and I was as it were submerged in a dream, a kaleidoscopic whirl of hallucinatory thoughtfulness through which my dream-life seeped into my thinking-life. In my haze I actually visualized the spiritual influence flowing as liquid smoke from the center of my sternum into my head.

And the doctors could find nothing physically wrong with me! Can you imagine? I awoke intermittently to hear them express their befuddlement to my landlord. (I have no precise idea how often they attended to me.) There was nothing the matter with me, they said. Nothing anyway their instruments could detect. Yet there I lay, quite obviously incapacitated. Of course they could not peer into my skull, but had their science provided them access to the interior of my mind, they would have seen my reason on fire, scorching itself and burning out. Or perhaps I should say, burning down the boundary between my intellect and imagination; burning down contemporary assumptions and perspectives; burning down all things timely and "sane." I recited verse in impossible meters on fantastic philosophical themes. I sang. I laughed. I gave voice to the madness that overwhelmed me. All this only in my head, you understand.

Shall I speculate that perhaps I descended into the underworld? But that would be outrageous. Let's say then that I lost myself in the labyrinth of the cave in the mind.

Strange to say, I emerged from this experience feeling better than I have of late, also with the sense of having attained a sort of insight. At the moment however my thoughts are but shadows of your own way of thinking, not yet integrated into the complex of my mind and mood. My hope is that through writing I shall make of them my own possession.

So. If you are right about truth and knowledge, if we agree that there is no truth, or at least that truth need not be our chief concern, nor knowledge our highest value, then we need not identify wisdom with knowledge, nor the love of wisdom, philosophy, with the search for truth. And if we reject the Christian imperative of correct belief, and Aristotle's assumption that the supreme function of intellect is to know, then we might well conclude that you are right. Further, if there is no God, or if the divine is not a jealous enforcer of orthodoxy, and if imagination is as proper to intellect as knowledge, then we may indeed draw that very conclusion. In which case we would be permitted—and maybe even compelled—to conceive of philosophy as a creative activity, and of the philosopher as one who through his artistry invents and explores new patterns of thinking and living. This would be the philosopher as poet and legislator, a type which you have mentioned in reference to Solon and Plato. He dreams the law of the future of man, and thereby he creates the future. His dream is his destiny. The past too: his longing and his will stretch even into the past.

But now I ask myself: Is this really the way things stand? Is this account of wisdom and the love of wisdom correct? More specifically, does it apply to Plato? Or, to put this question another way: Was Plato himself a Platonist? I have been reading the *Phaedo* lately, moved by your interpretive insights, and I am struck by many details which, of course, I have noted previously, but which I have never before strung together to read as you have done. How the dialogue opens up to reveal at its core Plato as an example of the type you have styled a "thinker-artist"! A Plato not obviously committed to Platonic dogma, who perhaps even means to subvert it!

Socrates in the *Phaedo*, when discussing the recurring dream which had often urged him to practice *mousikê*, which in the past he had taken as encouragement to continue practicing philosophy, says that he had recently considered whether it might not want him rather to compose poems. To this he was unaccustomed, he says, for the poet produces *mythoi*, not *logoi*, and he is not a teller of myths, a *mythologikos*. Yet on occasion throughout the work Socrates refers to his ideas as amounting to a *mythos*, and he prefaces the entire discussion by suggesting that he will *mythologein*, or tell a *mythos*, about life in the afterworld. As for the arguments, the *logoi*, which constitute the majority of the work, Socrates himself unsettles them in various ways. The first he introduces by proposing that they *diamuthologômen*, or relate a *mythos* about, the soul's immortality, which "myth" turns out to elaborate a *palaios logos*, or an ancient doctrine, an expression with roots in the mystery cults. Of the second argument, which encompasses much Platonic dogma—from the immortality of the soul to reincarnation and the doctrine that learning is recollection—he says that his *logos* holds only *if* Forms exist, but he offers no proof whatever that they do. And following the third argument he admits that many deficiencies, suspicions, and vulnerabilities yet remain. Later he even refers to his *logos* as a charm sung to frightened children and a noble idea worth the risk of believing. Why not affirm it as a demonstrably true account?!

In short, Plato seems determined to obscure the distinction between the philosopher and the poet which his Socrates insists on. More, as author of the words his characters speak, he as it were compels his Socrates to assert and then neglect the distinction, as if he would pit the old man against himself. (We have discussed his employing a similar tactic with the city-nature contrast at the start of the *Phaedrus*.) And even if he does not intend altogether to subvert Socrates' manner of philosophizing, he does at least call attention to himself as a type distinct from his protagonist. He is hinting at a lesson here, no? Weaving a message into the text, his enigmatic indication that he is something other than, *more* than, an ape of Socrates. The old man was a dry dialectician. Plato is beautiful and young (*kalos kai neos*), a thinker-artist whose philosophy cannot be untangled from his poetry.

Here I have only repeated facts that you know well, and conclusions which you have arrived at on your own already, I know. But, as I said, my intention in writing them down is to think them through and, perhaps, to incorporate them into my own ideas about these matters.

My ideas, yes, but also my emotions, for I recall your remarks on creativity as an affirmative reaction to suffering. As unwell as I was in my oblivion, I felt somehow relief, and a sort of peace. It was as if an ominous sun had set, a black star, a void that devours light. On its withdrawal a new horizon opened up before me, a new infinite, as it were, suffused with a radiance of liberation, exuberance, cheerfulness. I remember dancing... Not with legs, rather with my spirit... At the time I took this for an experience of approaching death, as one hears from pious aunts that peace descends on the dying as their departing souls are immersed in warmth and light. Therefore I dismissed the experience as the play of my subconscious making sense symbolically of my condition. Yet now I read it as a figurative image of the passing, not of life, but of death, the living-death suffered by those who accept their lives in the form prescribed by the timeliness of their time. The death of the father as the death of God. The death of God as a final release from bonds, intellectual and existential. That is to say, I experienced—if only briefly and through a shifting fog—I experienced the intellectual creativity of a mind set free from every cognitive constraint, thought wandering without limits, and life without negation, a profound mood for which every No! is itself an affirmation. If I was not the artist of my own thought-world, I was at least the promise of such artistry. Spirit radically unbound. As I write, my whole body shudders and smiles at the thought.

Shall I speak as you have done, then? Shall I say it with you? Indeed I shout it, I sing it, this charm of yours:

Nothing is true! Everything is permitted!

But enough of these scattered thoughts. I mean only to provide some indication of the recent trend of my thinking, if I may call it thinking rather than a dream-vision. And perhaps this is the proper designation, at least until I really think these things, for myself and as myself. As of now I fear I am only repeating sentiments borrowed from you. Yet I am confident that something of this way of thinking is authentically mine, or anyway bound to be so. I sense it moving in me, a spirit of life, new life, expanding through my frame.

Well then, as I say, Enough! With any other correspondent I would worry that this is far too involved a reply to a query into my well-being. But I don't doubt that you will understand and appreciate it. Besides, I have embedded in this narrative of my illness and recovery my contribution to our ongoing exchange. I await your reply.

In the meantime I continue my convalescence while pondering our investigative explorations. Of course I must also find the time to prepare and teach my classes, complete my latest research-essay, and attend to several pressing administrative matters... Ah, perhaps you are right, my friend, and the professor really does oppress the philosopher!

Charmides, the Younger

***

7 November

Friend Charmides,

I might have written sooner, but I thought to wait until the day on which Ficino with his Florentine Academy used to celebrate Plato's birthday. Who knows whether the date is grounded on hard fact? It makes no difference to me, my friend! Must we honor the great philosopher-artist as an historian who demanded of his admirers a rigid dedication to concrete actuality? No, of course not! Never! Therefore I begin by offering my lustiest *Auguri!* to the noble son of Ariston—or of Apollo, as the case may be.

And to you, too, my friend. *Tanti auguri di buon compleanno*, my dear Charmides! For I read in your most recent letter an account of a rebirth. Therefore I take this opportunity to hymn the virtues of the child, as I once promised I would do.

One must take advantage of one's second childhood. Most are not granted the experience, not anyway in any other than the superficial sense of the leisure years of those who survive to enjoy a dotage unburdened by the tedium of employment. Doubtless this is a state to which we all aspire. But here I mean to address the *childhood of the spirit* that comes upon those who transcend their youth and maturity alike, their ingenuousness as well as their grave solemnity. You describe your experience as the passing of death and the approach of life, indeed of *new life*. This strikes me as an appropriate formulation. The dawn of creative intellectuality, free from every cognitive constraint, and the exuberant affirmation of an unbound spirit. Yes, this really is new life and the childhood of the spirit. Or, as you say, your experience is at least the promise of this gift. It is set before you; now you must reach out and take it.

Youth is a mask that hides the young man from himself. The mask speaks. It says, "I am happy." Ah, but let us ask the man directly when as an adult he has been deprived of his disguise.

Old age is similarly deceptive. "I was happy," it says. And the lines across an old man's face resemble the mask of his youth redrawn from imperfect memory. It appears almost mournful.

Who among us is really happy, my friend? The simple-minded, I suppose. Most of the rest are sorrowful, dispirited, or blandly apathetic. Only the rare ones understand that our object is neither peace nor suffering. We few are after rather the *great health*. In this condition a man may as readily affirm his every spell of sorrow as disdain his happiness. For in this condition *great play* and *great seriousness* are intermingled in such a way as to drive the individual beyond concern with his fleeting emotional states. What are palpitations of the heart, quiverings of the lip, to such a one? Epiphenomena of the body, nothing more. Certainly nothing to distract us from our goal. And what exactly is our goal? The good, the beautiful, the true? Let us say: all of these and none, the difference depending on whether we conceive these categories from the perspective of the free-spirited philosophical artist or the pious metaphysician. Regarding them as so-called "transcendentals," the man of great health and a free spirit will have no use for them. Not anyway as does the Thomist, for example; not as a *true believer*. But as an artist he may well admire them; he may even be moved by them. But from a distance, my friend; always from a distance. For he does not permit his "self" to be entangled in such things. He is master of his every Yes and No. Describe him as believing or knowing if you like, but in either case he is actually *creating*. His will to know is a will to create.

This is what the child does, for this is what he is: a creator. The young and the old are pack animals, donkeys and distended camels, loaded down with the weight of tradition. In a word, they are believers. The child is a forgetting of tradition and a new beginning. Innocent but not naive. Pure but never prudish. He creates his own will, and he wills ever new creations. This is the primary sense in which his creative will is *free*.

This freedom of the great health is the object of the genuine philosopher's highest aspiration. Here is the innocence of the man who sports with the pious, the moral, the sacrosanct and the solemn with a skepticism deep but bright. He plays the *wicked* game with a *light* touch. He "knows" too much to believe. He is too "good" for virtue. The man who knows may disdain knowledge as no ignorant man has the *right* to do, and the man who has control of himself—of his emotions, desires, and behavior—may disdain morality too. Thus the childhood of the spirit is no mere given biological state. It is the reward for struggle, a condition which only the man who is safe around himself, and with himself, can risk the danger to attain and maintain. It is not for the weak of heart and mind, nor for the self-deceivers who mistake a decadent lust for license for free-spiritedness.

Reborn into the fertile childhood of his spirit, the philosopher-artist begets and gives birth within himself, his masculine seriousness a partner to his feminine playfulness. Thus does he generate thought-worlds, which burst from his internal potencies as stars sparking from out a chaos. His offspring are new realities and values: the real, the true, the good and the bad. Novel ways of life. The world we inhabit is fashioned by such men, men of the *vis creativa*, playfully creative types who resemble Heraclitus's cosmic king as a child playing at dice. The poem of our lives, for which the active types imagine themselves responsible, is in fact composed by men at play in the childhood of their spirit, men in whom the *vis contemplativa* is itself an active force. The "big-men" of the world, the supposed actors and originators of action, passively follow *our* script.

The spiritual child moreover is a Yes-sayer; he affirms his life, and the greater whole of which it is a part, all together as one. Consider the biological infant for a relevant parallel. The newborn experiences everything at once, and as one.

He makes no distinctions between himself and the world, nor among external objects. His reality is a fused and blurred mass. We can learn from this. I read in a newspaper the other day (forgive me, but I washed my hands afterwards) a column, which I take to be a weekly affair, in which the author reports several items of "good news" to remind his readers of "the true state of the world." But if he would really perform this service, should he not intermingle the good with the bad, the beautiful with the hideous? For is not the world at every moment a surge and a swelling of every species of act and event, the kind and the cruel, the graceful and vulgar, the merciful and the vengeful? Redemption is no more real, or "true," than crime, the warrior no less than the monk. Likewise with ideas. Here is Parmenides, there Heraclitus; here is Democritus, there Plotinus; and look, here too are Homer, Cicero, Dante, Shakespeare, Galileo, Hobbes, Goethe, Newton, Hume, and Kant. Ah, choosing sides is so tedious, the bluster of the "true" and the "false." I say: All things are always changing in every way, and yet everything always is at every moment. The one is in the many and the many in the one. Time and eternity. Being and Becoming. Enough! Dionysus is dismembered and restored. Forever. The frenzy never ebbs, never ends.

Let us then affirm this corybantic conglomerate, in its beauty and its brutishness. It is necessary after all—and in the end do we not wish some day to be Yes-sayers?

10 November, postscript

One last thought, my friend, before I post this letter. Let us pledge to recall on the occasion of our every birthday, as on all other days as well, the actual object of all our searching, wandering thoughts: ourselves. In the end we seek only ourselves. The people neither seek nor think; they simply "go along." The men of science think only superficially. The search for the fundamental atom, for mathematical proofs, for the truth of Plato's Forms, for universal ethical or aesthetic theories: the deeper thinkers understand that these are masks for other questions: Who am I? Why am I? But the deepest thinkers understand still more, namely that these latter questions are altogether unanswerable, and not from cognitive limitations, but rather because no answers are to be had, for nothing real corresponds to the expressions "the true self" and "the true meaning and purpose of existence." The questions which these others misformulate and conceal are: Toward what end am I living? Or, better: What shall I *make* of myself and my life? Who do I *will* to *become*?

Yes, my friend, we must take these matters into our own hands, for there are no facile and safe solutions to the problem of the universe, which is the problem of life, which is at base the problem, the mystery, of the so-called "I." But this problem, this mystery, is no puzzle to solve, to resolve or dissolve. Rather it is a labyrinth to experience and explore, boldly, with high-spirits and good-cheer. And this despite—no, not despite, but rather even *because of*—our understanding that the "I" is only a fiction, a serial epic poem. And we who are simultaneously the author and the actor of this work must construct a fluid self by fusing our Homer with our Achilles. Ah, let him who has ears hear, my friend. We must *live dangerously*!

VI

The Art of Philosophy

My friend and I met three more times following our first acquaintance. I returned to the mountains to visit him each of the next two summers, then once again the summer after the war began. (I never returned to the sanatorium except to walk the magnificent grounds.) By the second year of hostilities travel became so inconvenient, and at times so dangerous, as to be practically impossible. For years thereafter we maintained contact exclusively through the post. Until last summer, when finally I returned to the mountains to meet him again in person.

As I have mentioned in passing already, over the course of the intervening years I had thought my way into a novel manner and mode of philosophy. The events and ideas recorded in the 15 October letter reproduced in the previous chapter represent my first authentic insight into these matters. My friend had assessed me correctly: I didn't want to be a scholar who practices his craft on works of philosophy composed by other men. I aspired to be a philosopher myself, an authentic lover of wisdom. My scholarly training could aid me in this, for a philosopher requires a solid base of knowledge on which to build. But his distinctive activity does not consist of piling additional layers of information atop the existing structure. The typical scholar produces (I don't say that he "writes") articles and monographs. The philosopher blends acquired knowledge with elements of his own creativity to produce intellectual and existential works of art. Philosophy manifests in his mind, under his pen, and in and through his life.

Philosophy as a way of life. One encounters this phrase from time to time in commentaries on the ancients. The Hellenic schools of philosophy promulgated doctrine, but never as pure abstract theory dissociated from life. To join a school was to commit oneself to a particular manner of being in the world. One recognized a man as a follower of, say, Diogenes the Cynic from his bearing, his conduct, even his amusements and his clothes. Here we might employ a word of recent coinage and remark that each of the ancient schools advocated a "lifestyle." And the commitment was all-encompassing, for it engaged one's spiritual, intellectual, and ethical ideals.

The Platonists sought *likeness to God* through purification, the withdrawal of soul from bodily distractions and desires; the Peripatetics sought *eudaimonia* through cultivating the moral and intellectual virtues; the Epicureans sought *ataraxia* through the proper understanding of nature, the gods, life and death, and activities generative of simple refined pleasure. One could go on. Each of the schools posited a *telos*, an aim or end of human life conceived as the ultimate good, and they prescribed a method for attaining it. In one way or another the method entailed living by a specific canon of virtues. One flourishes by living virtuously. Thus when today we think of philosophy as a way of life, we tend to conceive of the "way" as having primarily to do with ethics or morality. The philosopher is committed to certain theoretical principles regarding reality and man, but even more than this he is committed to a virtuous life.

This conception of the philosophical life as primarily an ethical concern is valuable as far as it goes, I'm sure. But it does not go far enough.

I have often heard my friend complain that theories of aesthetics analyze beauty exclusively from the perspective of the viewer of a work of art, never from the perspective of the artist. Schopenhauer for example regards the experience of beauty as inducing in the viewer a state of calm detachment from the ceaseless striving of the will. He transcends phenomenal suffering, the wheel of Ixion stands still, and he contemplates pure Form as a pure will-less subject of knowledge. How different a state from the inspired frenzy of the artist! The artist is involved with beauty as one who labors to seduce, conceive, and give birth. He evokes beauty from the void, or rather he extracts it from his entrails. He loves, he dreams, he rages and despairs; he rushes about in a fever; he is madly enthused, then exhausted; he collapses; he slogs, he sweats, he is active. The viewer on the other hand is passive. He receives the work as a gift he has done nothing to deserve, and which perhaps he does not merit. He stands before it and admires; he contemplates it at his leisure. But does he comprehend it? Does he realize there is substance here to comprehend? That the work might well demand something of him? Not necessarily. Adrift in the peace which the work induces in his soul, he experiences nothing of the fire in which it was forged.

How then could one's conception of beauty not differ according to the perspective from which one regards it? "You must change your life," says the poet. But this sentiment stirs the man inspired to write it more profoundly than it moves the man who reads it. The former sings out with passion, the latter may only nod and blink his eyes, then return to his routine.

Our conception of philosophy as a way of life similarly approaches its object from the wrong direction. We may regard the philosophical life from the perspective of the student, the scholar, or the disciple, and there are no doubt advantages to doing so. But this parallels the approach to beauty solely from the perspective of the spectator, and it suffers from similar limitations. Surely there is greater value in conceptualizing philosophy from the perspective of the philosophical artist. If not for the aspiring academic, then at least for the aspiring philosopher. My friend once said to me, "I don't want to be a Platonist. I want to be a Plato." And with this remark he crystalized the distinction I am after here. The difference between regarding philosophy from the perspective of the scholar or disciple—the "spectator"—and from the perspective of the creatively generative philosopher—the "artist"—is the difference between learning how to be a Platonist and learning how to be a Plato.

Framing the matter this way makes sense of my friend's drive to track the traces of Plato the man imprinted on the texts of Platonic doctrine. There are those who turn to philosophy for guidance in the affairs of life. They require theories to accept, maxims to obey. They stand as students to the philosopher as professor, or as disciples to a guru. They require dogmatic content, therefore they treasure the text. But there are others who aspire to be philosophers themselves, not as followers, but rather as creators, as thinkers and writers, poets and legislators. Therefore they appreciate insight into the man, the philosopher behind the text, from whom they can learn what it means and what it takes—to become themselves an example of the type. And here we have the distinction between the devotee of philosophical doctrine and the philosopher as architect of a thought-world, which is to say the philosopher as a thinker-artist, to employ my friend's evocative expression.

Let us therefore regard the notion of philosophy as a way of life as bound up not, or not exclusively, with the choice between virtue and vice, but rather with the choice between a predominately investigative and a predominately creative life. The philosopher studies philosophical texts, to be sure, but not for the sake of mastering doctrine through objective analysis and precise interpretation. Rather he learns through study to think for himself. He reads the relevant scholarship, the more serious, rigorous, and pedantic the better, for the philosopher must be a "knower"; but he thinks, writes, and lives art, for above all else the philosopher is a *creator*. In short, the philosopher employs ideas and texts as stepping stones which lead to the core of his own unique spirit, and thereby to the conception of his own ideas and texts. The man who really lives philosophy, then, does not just live virtuously (he does this too, of course, though perhaps not in the conventional sense). He lives and acts in devotion to the Muses of his creative intellectuality; he makes of his soul a shrine to the deities of depth and beauty.

This, then, is the conception of philosophy as a way of life to which I attained some time ago. And for the past few years I have endeavored to live it out. Unfortunately, the busywork of a professor's routine constantly interferes. As an academic one must keep abreast of every development in one's field, no matter how ephemeral; one must contribute regularly to the ever-accumulating store of scholarship; one must publish in the appropriate journals and speak at prestigious conferences. And of course one must do all this while keeping up one's teaching duties, regardless whether one's classes relate to one's interests at any particular time. In brief, the business of working as a professor tends to obstruct one's every effort to live as a philosopher.

This sad fact would be the case even in the best of circumstances. But the farce into which my university has recently devolved has aggravated my particular problems. I have mentioned the extraneous busy-work imposed on faculty and staff by our administrative overlords. And I have reported my enraged reaction to it. Fortunately, despite numerous implied threats of retaliation, I suffered no serious repercussions. Perhaps a decline in the esteem and trust of my superiors, but considering their misplaced priorities, I took this as a compliment. This is not to say, however, that conditions in the institution improved. To the contrary, university administrators have carried on with their various asininities, have even compounded them to the point of parody.

In the immediate aftermath of the events recounted in the first chapter of this book, Senior Administration determined, in secret consultation with the Board, formally to implement unprecedented changes to the structure and curriculum of the university. This despite the fact that official regulations unambiguously decree that any such decision be approved by the University Council gathered in assembly. But money-men besotted with power often feel at liberty to ignore inconvenient regulations, and usually they act with impunity. They certainly succeeded on this occasion. Therefore it was promulgated as official university policy that the College of Liberal Arts, traditionally the heart of the institution, would henceforth function primarily as instructional support to the faculties of Law and Medicine, and to various of the natural sciences with military or commercial applications. Of course they took particular care not to express themselves as candidly as I have just done; rather they resorted to the standard bureaucratic half-truths and circumlocutions. But their intentions were evident nonetheless. To cite just one telling example, the core of required course distributions was radically restructured, so that the general student body would engage much less than previously with literature, history, and foreign languages, and in some cases not at all. In short, the university was now officially committed to catering to students who regard education exclusively as a mode of professional training.

I have called our administrators *philistines*. Did you think I was exaggerating?

This situation exacerbated the frustration and animus that seethed in me against the university's senior executives. The public collapse of the school's intellectual integrity, combined with my yearning to live unimpededly as a philosopher, daily intensified my desire to retire and withdraw into the mountains. Fortunately, the summer holidays were nearly upon us, at which time I could put these pressures out of mind and revisit the atmosphere in which I felt most at home.

I arrived in the mountains near the middle of June, not long after the late spring snows had melted away for good, and the meadows bloomed with life. Vibrant yellow flowers flourished everywhere, radiant and fragrant. I took a room in an old but comfortable hotel, and since I arrived in the early afternoon, after unpacking I left for a walk around the lake. I did not expect to encounter my friend, for we had not coordinated our arrival dates exactly, but I looked for him all the same. And with thoughts of the man's regal-whimsical personality revolving in my mind, I reflected on the differences between our ways of life, he the free-spirited philosopher-artist, I still fixed from day to day discontentedly enacting the role of philosophy professor.

I thought: one does well to compare the philosopher to the artist, to the poet, the painter, and musician. Otherwise one's only living exemplars of the type are academic scholastics and under-laborers of the sciences. But the philosopher is not an analyst, an accountant or technologist of ideas. His home is not the journal article. His aspiration is not security. Yet I fear that this is the end to which we are heading, or rather rushing, impetuously, recklessly. Having migrated to the university, and having begun thereby to mistake ourselves for members of a "profession," we philosophers are apparently eager to make ourselves over into specialists, micro-specialists even, captive to rigid and parochial modes of thought and action. Today we are in the process of becoming not just professors, which is bad enough, but professionals, which is worse.

None of this is to suggest that the philosopher should altogether neglect scholarship and science. The philosopher as a thinker-artist is more than simply an artist. He is a man of "knowledge," as I have said, even if he is not primarily a seeker of knowledge. Lacking expertise he would be but a dilettante or, worse, a charlatan, akin to a painter passing off a blank canvas for a meditation on the void. No, the philosopher is driven—he drives himself—to grind out the hard work. To endure it and enjoy it. His intellectual conscience bites deep. But his creative spirit is a match in power. Free play with the product of his labor is reward for force expended.

Let's say then that the lover of wisdom is an artist whose medium is the idea expressed in words, and whose subject matter is resident in the traditional canon of philosophy. This includes of course the questioning and reevaluation of the canon. I am tempted to maintain that the philosopher is one for whom the nature of philosophy, and his own activities as a philosopher, are of paramount concern; that he himself is the primary object of his inquiry, including himself as inquirer, and therefore including even the terms of his inquiry; and that as a consequence he is constantly in danger of losing himself in a self-referential infinite regress of questions and replies, yet at every moment he centrifugally resists collapse into the singularity. In sum, that a philosopher in his spirit is this constant play of instability and recovery of balance. In the best of cases the result resembles a dance.

My second day in the mountains I still did not encounter my friend. I walked our favorite paths, circled the lake in the morning and again that afternoon, but to no avail. Early in the evening I sat to observe the sunset from his favorite bench. Sparrows darted excitedly over the meadows, climbing, diving, feeding on tiny insects. The wildflowers bowed and huddled together against the chill approach of night. The waters of the lake darkened and lay solemnly still. And with the overlooming mountains conjuring thoughts of altitude and ascent, I reflected glumly on my own stagnation on the horizontal planes of life. Then once again I thought of the artist, the man for whom advancement and ascension are perpetual inspirations.

The true artist flows like Becoming personified, for he thrives as who and what he is through ceaseless displacement and change. Not by chance, but intentionally, for stasis is the eternal foe of every creative spirit. Call it a propensity to boredom if you will, but the greatest artists are the boldest revolutionaries, forever overthrowing their own ideals, even their own inclinations and drives. They experiment with methods, techniques, and styles; they explore themselves; they master their craft. Then suddenly, remarkably, they change direction, sometimes to the horror of their admirers, to the horror even of that part of themselves that feels settled and at ease. Something within the artist senses that settled ease is the death of creativity, the cessation of all accomplishment. In logical terms we might call the artist's tendency to revolution a form of "inconsistency." Well then, so much the worse for logic and consistency!

Now why should philosophers deny themselves the pleasure of ascent and the joy of creative intellectual revolution? Fear of violating disciplinary boundaries? Fear of the bogeyman of validity? Is the philosopher then a coward? Let's say that the typical philosopher is a slave to reason. He regards it as his business, his professional academic concern, to formulate arguments or theories to defend against all rivals. He lavishes his theories with greater care than he gives to himself. The truth is more valuable than the man, he says. He is a "truth-seeker."

A truth-seeker? Wherefore? And if I myself am the man whose value is at issue? No, no. I say: to the devil with this pious reverence for consistency and objectivity, as if logic were truth and truth were divine. Life itself is the highest value of a living organism—in my own case, *my* life, and the truth be damned.

On my deathbed I shall give no thought to whether any one of my pet ideas has been proven finally and irrefutably true. I shall want to review my past and affirm with confidence that mine was a rich, rowdy, expansive, profound, joyful, intellectually creative life. And I hope that with my last breath I shall pronounce an exuberant Yes! to life, to *my* life. To my ideas, too, of course; but not primarily to their "truth-value." Rather to their beauty, to the grace of their companionship, to the favor of their arrival and even of their leave-taking. I do not dismiss the truth as altogether without value, for the artist dips his brush in every color as it suits his mood. The philosopher-artist too. Yet I shall always subordinate truth to life, never my life to truth. For my ultimate aim is neither correspondence nor confirmation, but experience, adventure, growth, ascent. Really, I just want to feel *alive*.

Consider these matters in the context of pure art. The Impressionists did nothing to prove the validity of their vision. Monet provided no argument for the soundness of his water lilies, nor did Pissarro expose fallacies in proposed refutations of his haystacks. Artistic revolutions do not hinge on proof. Rather, the Impressionists gave their peers permission to explore new modes of perception and novel techniques of painting. They sanctioned the insurrection by their very act of rebelling.

Similarly, the philosopher as revolutionary does not require proof—as if any man has ever strictly proven anything of interest in this world. At most the philosopher requires permission, the sanction to follow his Muse no matter its eccentric deviations from tradition, the follies intermingled with its seriousness. And as among the artists, the highest manifestation of the type *philosopher*, the creator as opposed to the follower, will provide his own sanction. Will *be* his own sanction. His permission is his boldness, his recklessness even, for the tradition he most opposes resides within. He takes up arms against himself to serve himself; reverberations in the external world are after-shocks of this central act. He himself, in heart and mind, is his master-piece. Never complete yet fulfilled at every moment.

Days passed and still my friend did not turn up. I must say I began to worry. I wrote his associate in Basel but received no reply. Had I known where he stayed when in town I would have made inquiries there, but he took a different room with every visit. The particularities of his personality were such that he was forever on the hunt for the ideal residence, a house or hotel superior to the one he'd selected the previous summer, a less expensive place with a warmer room, or with higher ceilings, with larger windows or a balcony, or quieter—silence was essential—a bright, quiet room with a comfortable chair and a desk for writing.

"Well," I told myself, "I've reserved my room for two full months. He will arrive before I leave." I expected him any day. In the meantime, I went out of my way to modify my usual patterns of thought and action. I eschewed professional work and passed my time outdoors, walking, thinking, exercising my imagination. I composed songs and poems then immediately forgot them; I wrote essays in experimental styles; I indulged my daydreams. All with an eye toward freeing myself from encrusted scholarly habits. Eventually I settled down to compose a short work of intellectual autobiography which centered on my relationship with Plato, part fact, part fantasy, a philosophical fever-dream recorded as a prose-poem. It wasn't meant to be great. It was different, exploratory, liberating, and that was the point. It was valuable as therapy, as a reorienting rehabilitation.

For these and other creative-intellectual experiments I drew inspiration from Plato's *Phaedo*, which I read afternoons on my friend's bench in the meadow before the lake. In the past I had concentrated exclusively on the dialogue's *logoi*, evaluating the arguments for immortality, analyzing the concluding account of the Forms as causes. Now following my friend's example I ignored these matters and experienced the piece as a complex work of art, as a mountain of a *mythos*. What a strange and beautiful artifact! Strict Platonic dogma on the surface, Plato the playful thinker-artist winkingly peeking out from behind the scenes. Imagine an academic today composing a treatise on the soul which included so much apparently superfluous material, allusions to the Minotaur and Dionysus, Apollonian themes of harmony and the prophetic songs of dying swans, a detailed description of the afterworld and the "true earth," repeated intimations that the arguments are unsound or incomplete. No respectable press would publish such a work. What's the genre? Who's the audience? What exactly is the point? I can only infer that for Plato the arguments were not the point, or anyway not the central point.

Plato understood the limitations of argument. He proved it time and again in his so-called aporetic dialogues, representations of dialectical exchanges which end without resolution. Even his great dialogue on knowledge—the *Theaetetus*, also included in the volume of the *Platonis Dialogi* which my friend had often with him—concludes with the stalemate of aporia. The interlocutors cannot define knowledge, much less provide an account of the proper method of attaining it.

Plato's Academy became officially a skeptical institution less than a century after the master's death when Arcesilaus was elected scholarch. Inspired by Plato's portrait of Socrates in the aporetic works, Arcesilaus maintained that since we lack a secure criterion of truth, knowledge is altogether inaccessible. Specifically, he contended against the Stoics that no sense impression is self-validating, for we cannot rule out the possibility of false impressions which resemble the truth in every detail. In brief, any one of our perceptions, no matter how clear and distinct, may for all we know be false, and we have no criterion to distinguish the true from the false perceptions.

Later skeptics, particularly those in the Pyrrhonian tradition, insisted that even logic and reason are subject to this so-called "problem of the criterion," for of any argument we may inquire respecting its ultimate justification. Even granting that the conclusion follows from the premises, the question remains whether the premises are true. A dialectician may arbitrarily assume the truth of his premises, but assumptions are not demonstrations of truth. Another may attempt to demonstrate the truth of his premises by deriving them from the conclusion which the premises are meant to prove, but this results in a viciously circular argument. Yet another may avoid circularity by deriving his premises from premises independent of the conclusion at issue, but in this way he only defers the problem, for we may inquire into the criterion which justifies these new premises. And if in his reply he resists the urge to assume their truth arbitrarily, or to employ a circular argument, he will have to derive them from still other independent premises, in which case we shall then inquire after *their* criterion. And so on *ad infinitum*. In sum, then, the Pyrrhonian contends that the conclusion of every argument depends on premises whose truth is either hypothesized without proof, derived by way of fallaciously circular reasoning, or ultimately indemonstrable because subject to an infinite regress, which is to say that no conclusion is ever finally justified.

But if neither sense impressions nor argumentation can secure the truth, it would seem that nothing can. Nor will it help to appeal to the results of scientific investigation (more and more the popular appeal these days), for science no less than other forms of reasoning relies on sense impressions and argumentation. And even if we set aside every general skeptical objection, there are many specific arguments against the particular methods and claims of the sciences.

We might note, for example, that even the most successful of past scientific theories have in time been abandoned for more comprehensive, mathematically simpler, or more fruitful theories, from which we may infer that even the most successful of our current theories will suffer the same fate. Call this a pessimistic induction on the history of science.

Nor should we assume that any presently successful theory is true at least until it has been shown to fail, for neither practical nor theoretical success is proof of truth. Even false theories produce results. Hence the so-called "Instrumentalists" conceive of theories as tools, or instruments, which empower us to manipulate the world, but which have as little to do with truth as does a thumb or a wrench, which also empower us to manipulate our world.

Then there are those who argue that no rigorously scientific claims can be either verified or falsified, for propositions expressing universal laws must by definition assert more than finite experience can verify, and one may always redirect the force of falsifying observations from the specific hypothesis at issue to some other component of the broader theory.

There are even scholars who from the study of the historical record of actual scientific practice conclude that there is no uniform scientific method, nor any results derived exclusively from specifically scientific practices. Science as the theoretical construct one encounters in the textbooks may on paper appear an ideal resource for acquiring knowledge, but science as actually practiced is messier than this, and often even tangled up with unscientific assumptions and procedures.

Finally there are the Pragmatists, who advocate deflating or altogether abandoning our traditional notions of truth, reality, and the so-called "correspondence" relation supposed to obtain between true beliefs or propositions and the world, a relation which no one to date has satisfactorily explained.

All this is to say that for every claim to knowledge there are counter-claims of ancient or modern pedigree to oppose them. None of these arguments amounts to a proof against the possibility of knowledge or truth, yet we may appeal to them for permission to withhold assent from any particular claim to truth with which we are confronted. The general idea is consonant with the Pyrrhonian position, namely that for every argument there exists an equipollent counterargument, and that given the balance of plausibility one ought to suspend judgment.

I have described the philosopher with reference to the artist as one who gives himself permission to experiment with ideas, even to mount revolutions against his own mind. In this, skepticism is his ally. For if nothing can be definitively known to be true, every idea is permitted. Only the three-fold belief that truth exists, that we know the truth, and that we have epistemic or moral obligations to honor the truth can restrict our freedom to engage at will in creative-intellectual exploration and innovation. I have come to call the position that aims to undermine this belief for the sake of a free-spirited mode of philosophy, "Creative Pyrrhonism."

Not every man is suited for this creative application of Pyrrhonism. For the timidly indecisive, skepticism may be a symptom of exhaustion, the expression of a nihilistic resignation and denial of the will to affirm and negate. For the genuine philosopher, on the other hand, skepticism is the expression of a spirit dangerously uninhibited yet severe enough to resist the lure of degenerate license, the spirit that rises above belief and unbelief as master of its every Yes and No. With reference to the adherent of this audacious skepticism, we may say of Creative Pyrrhonism that the Pyrrhonian element clears the ground, the creative element promotes free play in the open space of the clearing.

Six weeks into my stay in the mountains I concluded that my friend was not coming. I had never known him to arrive so late in the season. He might surprise me yet, of course;

but I no longer expected him. I could only hope that he was well and lament the absence of so inspiring a personality.

As for myself and my own condition, although I had come to take the cure under my friend's care (so to speak), I sensed that I now possessed the charm to heal myself. I had suffered no headaches since arriving in the mountains, and while formulating my conception of the philosopher as a Creative-Pyrrhonist and thinker-artist my mood improved distinctly, as manifested in a cheerfulness in my bearing and a lightness in my step, despite the seriousness of my purpose. I walked for hours every day, a notebook and pencil in my jacket pocket to record my thoughts, and under my arm my copy of the *Platonis Dialogi*, volume one. I read the *Phaedo* daily, as I have said, perusing the text with the fastidiousness of an old philologist and the daring of an artist, a Theseus of hermeneutical exploration. The dialogue was my labyrinth, doctrinal Platonism the Minotaur stalking the text, and insight into Plato himself as the playfully serious philosopher-artist would be my prize for slaying the beast of dogma. My friend's inspiration was my Ariadne's thread, and my adaptation of his perspective to my own intellectual and existential needs was my bronze sword.

One further source of my flourishing health and high spirits was the fact that I had finally resolved to resign from my university. Mine will be an early retirement, for I am still relatively young. But I am fortunate to be the beneficiary of a modest family inheritance, which together with my other savings and a small pension should sustain me in a modest life for years to come. I decided to teach for one more year, for I had obligations to various students whose futures were of concern to me, and I did not like to abandon my colleagues without providing them sufficient opportunity to replace me. But the matter was conclusively settled in my mind, and with the promise of emancipation finally having been pledged, I felt as if I were already free.

At lunch one day near the end of my stay I reflected on the several decisions I had recently taken, particularly my determination finally to incorporate my new way of thinking into my way of life. It occurred to me then that these developments would provide a suitable theme for a new philosophical composition, resembling the intellectual autobiography I had recently composed, but less stylistically experimental and more straight-forwardly substantive. In the moment sitting over my meal the inspiration was overwhelming. Unfortunately, I had neglected when leaving my room to take my notebook from my desk. I had a pencil in my pocket but no paper on which to write. Therefore I asked the waiter for a clean sheet from his notepad, and when he gave it to me I covered it front and back with a detailed outline of this book, which is to say this very book that you are now reading. I revised the substance in minor particulars while writing at home during this past academic term (my last!), but now that the work is nearly complete I see with pleasure that I have more or less adhered to my original conception. In any case, the writing of this outline amplified my good mood, and after placing the folded paper in my jacket pocket I hurried out for a long walk without returning to my room. That night I slept more soundly than I had in years, deeply content with my station and condition.

The next morning I awoke excited about my new project, and I went out for an early walk on the grounds of the sanatorium to ruminate on the work. This time I did not forget my notebook. I filled a page with commentary supplementary to my outline, and for the next several days I kept to this routine. Immediately after breakfast I would circle the grounds of the sanatorium then cross the meadow toward the lake and sit for a while on my friend's bench, thinking, reading, and writing, then circle the lake and pause again on the bench before returning to my room to nap before lunch. Viewed from above, my course traced out a lemniscate, the figure-eight curve which symbolizes infinity, and which has also been employed to depict the ouroboros. I took this as significant of the self-reflectivity of the philosophical life, the love of wisdom which by continually streaming out perpetually surges into itself.

Constant meditation on the *Phaedo* inspired my decision to present my own work as a fiction. I had come to associate Plato's greatest dialogues more closely with, for example, Homer's *Iliad*, Michelangelo's *Pietà*, and Beethoven's symphonies than with Aristotle's *Physics* or Kant's first *Critique*. Or rather I should say that Plato's works spring from the masterly combination of all these styles. Not as the output of a decadent motley type, but rather as the self-expression of history's first *capacious soul*. Plato was a rare amalgamation of those grand types to which Pythagoras, Sophocles, and Thucydides belonged. Most great spirits are one type or the other—the thinker *or* the artist—which makes them pure but limited, and therefore ultimately exhaustible. Plato on the other hand approaches the infinite:

his thought flows into his art, his art floods through his thought, in a perpetual cycle of mutually infusing enrichment. Therefore his work is inexhaustible, ultimately unfathomable, and, to state the obvious, quite the opposite of boring.

Needless to say it is not my intention to compare my work to Plato's, no more than to associate the consequence with the source of inspiration. The dialogues moved me to explore my every resource of creativity, and to interweave my artistry with my intellect. It may well be that here the similarity ends. I can live with that, for the person I have come to be through this interweaving is a man with whom, and *as* whom, I am happy to live.

In any case, as I say, I conceived this little book last summer, near the end of my most recent sojourn in the mountains. Call it a memorial to my friend, or to myself as I was healed through the influence of his charm. Or both: for as I remarked at the commencement of my story, these days it is hard to make such nice distinctions. And perhaps it is worth noting here, as I conclude this final chapter, that I very nearly did not write this book, not anyway in its present form. I almost lost the outline—or rather I did lose it, only to have it returned to me.

One morning as I sat on my bench gazing out over the lake, my volume of Plato beside me, and thoughts of the *Phaedo* as philosophical art spiraling through my mind, I sensed a presence in my peripheral vision. There beside me stood a man whom I had seen in passing on my last few walks, his arm outstretched and in his hand a folded piece of paper. He had observed it fall from my pocket as I withdrew my notebook while walking toward the lake, he said.

I took the paper and inspected it, and of course I recognized it immediately. My outline! I had almost lost it forever! You can imagine how thankful I was for the man's kindness. I stood up and shook his hand, smiling broadly and expressing my infinite gratitude, so hard-won were the thoughts I'd recorded there, so vital to my well-being, past and future alike. And in that present moment, too, naturally.

Epilogue

I sit down to compose this coda to my story having just arrived home from my office. For the last time. Before departing I slipped my letter of resignation into the campus mail bin outside my office door. I don't doubt that from time to time I'll return to visit colleagues and old friends, or to make use of the library, but never again as an employee. My days "on the job," as they say, are over. *Vado in pensione*, as my friend would put it. I am going into retirement. Not to dawdle and grow old—I hope this goes without saying— but rather quite the opposite. At last I shall be at liberty to work, my kind of work, my avocation, what I now understand to be my authentic vocation: to think, to write, to live as a philosopher, no longer merely as a professor of philosophy. I figure that since I'm retiring young, I might just manage the thing while I still have time to appreciate it.

Walking home this afternoon I took my usual route, recalling along the way my impressions from last winter as I've recorded them in this book. The city and its busy denizens, materialistic conventionalists all, their spirits distracted and dissipated by the basest forms of feeling and thinking, by bogus religion, sentimentality, mass-marketing, and journalism (all of which amount to the same thing)— this hurry-scurry modern city life, which has lost all connection to nature and to the world as it was before the arrival of industry and technology, before our infatuation with the Now!—this scene still repels me. Yet every day I strive to maintain my equilibrium. As Epictetus advised, he who visits the baths should expect to be splashed. I want no longer to let the tumult disturb me. I want no longer to be disturbed at all. Therefore I am determined henceforth to avoid the raucous bathhouse of contemporary culture.

I am going into the mountains.

Throughout the entirety of this, my last year as a professional academic, I have practiced at calmly turning away from the various social, cultural, political, and institutional absurdities that have exercised me in the past. I meditate on the proposition that each act and every event is an element in the construct that is this world, the whole, and to that extent at least each one is necessary. What then is the point of butting one's head against these things? One's reward at best is a migraine. No, from now on I don't want to accuse; turning away shall be my only negation.

Above all else it is necessary that I turn away from the dying university. The institution in its death throes will thrash about for another fifty years, at least, before its final dissolution. One could stay on without suffering overmuch. But for those with ears to hear, the death-rattle is audible even now. It is a horrible sound, and I want no more of it.

In the mountains I shall find silence, and avoid intellectual contamination. I am going, then, not to run away, not to withdraw exclusively into myself alone, to live as a hermit, bitter and brooding, a fugitive from reality. Rather, my turning away from the busy-ness and baseness of the world shall be a turning toward myself. In the mountains I shall cultivate a pathos of distance in an atmosphere that inspires me to plumb my depths and scale my heights. I shall commune with nature. I shall have space in which to breathe, pure air circulating through my lungs, and time to savor the life-force surging through me. I shall walk; I shall wander; I shall think and write. In short, in the mountains I shall come to myself as if I were meeting a stranger destined to become a friend.

At the start of this year I informed my colleagues of my intention to retire; I spoke also with those students whose work I am presently supervising (as I shall continue to do by way of correspondence). As far as I know they have all been true to their word to keep the matter to themselves. My superiors will be surprised, but I don't mind to inconvenience the bureaucratic managers. Let them work for their inflated salaries. Besides, they will have no trouble replacing me. When the youngest of my colleagues finally retires, however, they likely won't even bother filling the vacancy. By then the vulgar technocrats will have driven liberal learning into whatever cramped corner remains unoccupied by training in the professional trades. Little need in that bleak future for the hiring of fresh young humanists.

In time I suppose even the philosophers will succumb. Future students schooled in philosophy will not regard themselves as lovers of wisdom, but rather as applicants seeking entry into a profession. And when at last no lovers of wisdom remain, but only members of the "philosophy profession," then philosophy will have finally died, at least as practiced in the university.

To be honest, I admit that in my career as an academic I myself have contributed to the debasement of philosophy. Consider my professional activities to date. I have made my reputation analyzing arguments, occasionally by adding to the ever-swelling store of scholarly minutiae. I have written articles and monographs aimed exclusively at my peers. To stake out and defend a position, to refute my opponents, to prevail in the petty contest of academic disputation. I have moreover written, not for the creative act of writing, but rather to produce a text and be done with it. I have been in a hurry. I have not written in order to think, or to imagine, or to inspire, but rather to be read, reviewed, admired. To exert an influence on my field.

Of course I did not regard myself and my activities so disparagingly at the time, but now that I have adopted an intellectual perspective infused with the demands and delights of creativity, the fact stands out in retrospect as obvious. I have flourished because I am after all sincere in my love of wisdom, but I have been unwell because my love and my conception of wisdom have for years been perverted by the assumptions inherent in the profession through which I pursued them.

But this present book I've approached much differently than any of my previous works. I have altogether avoided my usual routine. No strict writing schedule. No stress; no hurry. I have taken my time. Six months, in which span in the past I have written books over twice as long as this. But did I enjoy my writing of them? Was the activity a pleasurable indulgence? Did it lift me up into a state of contemplative-creative cheerfulness? I did enjoy myself, as a matter of fact; but my pleasure was shot through with anxiety. I was eager to draw my inferences and to state my final conclusions. I counted the days. Today I come to the end of this work thoroughly relaxed. I contemplate each paragraph, the sentences and individual words even, as a painter stepping back from a canvas admires the colors coating his hands almost as much as he cherishes the painting itself. Today, in short, I am at my ease.

As for my health, I haven't suffered a serious headache in well over a year. Not one since finally resolving to retire; and over the course of my acquaintance with my friend, the frequency and intensity of my pains have steadily diminished. My melancholia persists, alas, and I suspect it always will. One doesn't rid oneself of this condition as physicians eradicate a virus with vaccines. One must apply one's philosophical charm daily, hourly even. I have come to understand that one dark vein of melancholy need not spoil the marble of joy through which it runs. One must learn to work with it, as a sculptor works with an impurity exposed in the stone from which he strives to extract his vision of the beautiful. To affirm one's life, even in its every mani-festation, one need not experience only highs and happiness. One must learn to appreciate, and benefit from, even one's suffering. One must adopt a lofty perspective from the summit of which one affirms events which the self as immediately involved with them decries.

I am reminded of my father, the lamentable figure of a dissatisfied man. As gifted as he was in many ways, he never did master the art of giving style to his character, of taking himself in hand and imposing his will on his life. His virtues and vices tyrannized over him; he was a slave to his Yes and No. In short, he was not in control of himself. Looking back, I believe that I intuited this even as a child, though I could not have articulated it then. Rather, it manifested in my consciousness as a mystified confusion at my father's character and deeds, and later as a diffuse sadness spreading out from the man at its center to shade the wider world grey.

He who grows up troubled by indistinct suspicions about his father may develop distorted perceptions and self-conceptions. These may be to his benefit or his disadvantage, depending on his creative power to bend them to his own will and purpose. In my case, the experience implanted in my spirit the seed of an aspiration to flourish with the great health of the man who is master of his virtues and his vices, who dictates to his affirmations and denials, the type who puts his strengths and weaknesses to his use, not the other way around, and who rules himself in accord with a plan expressive of a unified taste, artistic and existential. This constraint of style was evident in my father's craftsmanship, but his life was all too often arbitrary and disorderly. He failed to balance his instinct with a cultivated intellect; his melancholy was unleavened with cheerfulness; and his spirit was corrupted by forces beyond his comprehension. Therefore he suffered, and, as I have said, he succumbed eventually to nihilism.

Now consider in this light the historical Charmides, after whom my friend was fond of calling me. Who knows whether he overcame his own suffering? It is certain at least that Socrates' charm did not cure him of his lustful self-indulgences. Notoriously, he profaned the scared rites of the Eleusinian Mysteries in a drunken debauch with the profligate Alcibiades, and he died defending the corrupt regime of the so-called Thirty Tyrants. Rather than become the cultivated philosopher-poet of his youthful aspiration, he embraced the nihilism latent in the ideas of sophists like his cousin Critias. However many, and however intense, the bodily pleasures he enjoyed, I doubt his spirit ever found peace or genuine cheerfulness.

I don't mean to condemn the sophists' ironic perspective on value and knowledge, which to some extent I share. Rather, I intend to reflect on the supplementary elements necessary to avoid a permanent descent into nihilism. The philosopher must not flee nihilism, but neither should he employ it as excuse to indulge his basest impulses. Nor of course should he sit down in the midst of it, impotent and despairing. The man who would make his way to wisdom must push through to the far side of nihilism, he must live through the whole of it, then leave it behind and outside himself. But for this he must infuse his spirit with the philosophy of life, and his philosophy with the spirit of art.

Therefore I am going into the mountains, for there this variety of free thinking and free living, this wickedly free free-spiritedness, is still possible. One aspires to a higher state than either pious belief or nihilistic unbelief, and the philosopher as poet and legislator, the philosopher as a thinker-artist, may provide an example here. Consider Plato, the paradigmatic instance of the type: like all great artists Plato was something of a cosmic demiurge, a creator of a thought-world. His idiosyncratic collection of concepts and ideas generated an organizing perspective on reality, and since the world itself is constructed through the human perspectival contribution, his system summoned into being a cosmos of experience.

Creative activity on so grand a scale does not depend on belief, nor is it undermined by unbelief. One does not construct a thought-world by gathering an assortment of propositions approved for use through empirical confirmation. Propositions, beliefs, and evidence are irrelevant here. To be frank, I no longer understand what a belief is meant to be in this context. A cognitive attitude toward a proposition? I say this is empty talk. One inhabits and is inhabited by a *Weltanschauung*, one's experience is shot through with the ideational content of one's mind, and the world itself just is this experience. There is neither harmony nor opposition of mind and world. There is only the singular thought-world: this is our "reality."

I have noted that during my stay in the mountains last summer I studied Plato's *Phaedo* closely. I read it again this past Christmas holiday, in preparation for the writing of this book. This time I engaged with the work as one engages with a poem or novel. I lingered over the text as one lingers over a work of art, stunned by the mystery, savoring the beauty, overwhelmed by the wonder of it all. On this reading a surprising new detail came suddenly into view. It may be that I have read more into it than is warranted by the facts, but at the moment the inspiration matters more to me than accuracy of interpretation. The notion of wisdom as *phronêsis* appears throughout the text, but *sophia* occurs only twice, both times ironically. First it is the "wisdom which they call the inquiry into nature," an inquiry that employs a method which Socrates dismisses as futile and confusing.

Later, *sophia* is the "cleverness" of the *antilogikoi*, the disputatious intellectuals who entangle their opponents with words. This set me to thinking: what if wisdom is only a word, not an actual state? In the *Apology* Socrates speculates that he is wiser than other men because he does not think he knows what he does not know. But this suggests that "wisdom" is nothing like an accumulated store of knowledge, that it is instead the absence of pretension, which is to say a negative condition, nothing of active substance in itself. It suggests, in short, that there is no such thing as wisdom as an intellectual or spiritual state in and of itself. But if this is so, what then shall we say of philosophy, *eudaimonia*, and objective moral virtue? Might these too be mere words and phrases, meretricious conceptual finery draped over a void? And what of the other exalted concepts admired by the philosophers, even by myself? What if we are chasing phantoms? What if all there really is, and all there really needs to be, is *thinking* and *life*?

At all times and everywhere the pondering man stands out. He blithely declines to participate in the faddishness of mass-life, even in the trends that reign among the intellectual classes. Thus his fellows reach for a word with which to label him. "What is he after?" they wonder. "Let us call him *philosophos*, a lover of wisdom, a seeker of *sophia*, for all this thinking must be directed toward some end. No one thinks just to think. No one does anything solely for its own sake. That would be impractical, and man is nothing if not the practical animal." And thus are the notions of *sophia* and *philosophia* born, words floating free of any objective correlative.

Similarly with the pondering man's way of life. Most men yearn to profit from existence, as if they would not act, could not survive, without a guarantee of the propriety of their actions and the promise of a cosmic reward. They want more than the preponderance of pleasure over pain, more even than the cheerfulness that accompanies a beautiful existence. They want a *good life*. More, they want *the* good life, or at least the assurance that such a determinate condition is attainable. In short, they crave objectivity and certainty. They cannot affirm their lives unless they believe that "Yes" is somehow the right answer, an absolute truth inscribed in the stars or in the mind of God.

But, as I say, I sometimes wonder whether all this is just so much gaseous bombast and delusion, a grand conceptual fabrication designed to mask the groundlessness of human life and thought. Mind you, I don't insist that *sophia*, *eudaimonia*, and other such philosophical concepts are a sham, for I don't presume to know. My point is only that sometimes I suspect as much, and that if this is so indeed, I can be content all the same. For these days I try not to fret over whether I shall ever discover the Truth, act always in accord with the Good, or satisfy an academic taxonomist's definition of Philosophy. Instead I endeavor to live an abundant, thoughtful, creative, exuberant life.

I don't want to argue over labels. I am content to call myself a pondering man or thinker-artist, and to leave "philosopher" to the academics, if that will make them happy. Whatever it is I have accomplished through this book, you may call me after that.

Reflecting on my association with my friend in the Val di Sogno, I realize now that as much as I learned from him, in the end I sought only myself through him. He was to me a purifying mirror. This insight recalls a conversation during which my friend once said to me that underlying all else we do is the *ricerca interiore*, the internal search. The scientist, the spiritual disciple, and the adventurer on the high seas— every seeker, without exception, no matter the immediate concrete object of his search, is really after himself alone. All the rest is distraction and diversion, a skittering across the surface of life.

This is not to say that we should abandon the objects of our superficial searches, that we should not allow ourselves, perhaps for years on end, to ignore, neglect, even outright to repudiate the deeper search for ourselves. To the contrary, the apparent diversion from our actual search may well be integral to it. In moving away one draws near. For a time anyway. Eventually, however, one must stand honestly before oneself and acknowledge the distractions for what they are: deferrals. Then one must turn intentionally toward the authentic search for the proper goal. One must make the inward turn, or incorporate into one's inwardness even everything external.

On this model of interior exploration, the seeker's aim is not self-knowledge in a strict metaphysical sense. One need not assume the existence of a "self," of self as substance, as stable and essentializing nature, to respect the Delphic *gnôthi sauton*. The idea of self may be of value even if it designates only a fluid and shifting thing, with no enduring nature, a moving play of surfacing and dissipating, aligning and dissociating, ephemeral forces.

Nor should we misconstrue the "knowledge" at issue here. To borrow from my friend, in the man of great health the will to know is a will to create. As an interior explorer, in the bloom of the childhood of his spirit, he is no cold scientist intent on objectivity and truth. He seeks no anteriorly existing "I," fully formed, pre-defined, waiting to be discovered. Rather, he finds himself by creating himself; he becomes who he is through an ongoing act of artistic-intellectual will.

One seeks moreover to befriend oneself, seeks self-experience, self-communion, internal amity, peace. Do we not after all from time to time suspect that we are strangers to ourselves, and that if we should meet ourselves on the road we would look upon the mirrored image un-recognizingly? That we might even confront ourselves with hostility, bewilderment, surprised admiration, or blank indifference? A wanderer alien to his shadow? All this is indeed the case; of course it is. We don't need objective knowledge of a metaphysical self to grasp these truths about ourselves. Much more urgently we require a healing, a charm that is a cure.

I began this book by stating that I returned to the mountains to find my friend. That was last summer, and as I reported in the previous chapter, my search was un-successful. I hope to find him this year. But if not, I will anyway have found the way to friendship with myself, which is incalculably more significant.

And so now I am done, with this book, and with this phase of my life. But this is just to say that now at last I shall begin to live. But not here, not in the hubbub of the modern city, with its shallow culture and dying universities. I am leaving all this behind. I am returning to nature, ancient and profound. I am going into the mountains.

THE END

Editor's Note

Michael Tommasi, much like his imagined narrator, abandoned the frenetic modern world for a long, thoughtful residence in the mountains. He did not retreat to Switzerland, however, but rather to Mystras, the Byzantine hill-town perched atop an imposing spur of the Taygetos mountains overlooking Sparta. An ideal setting for a pondering man, an atmosphere sublime. I wonder: Have you ever stood beside the Menelaion on the ridge across the way, gazing at this purple chain of peaks stretched out for miles like the fossilized spine of the Peloponnese, the broad Laconian plain below, the Eurotas river glimmering under a cloudless azure sky? Have you experienced the mystic beauty of this scene, the profundity of nature and history harmoniously resounding? Then you will understand how it was that ancient Sparta bred such poets, lawgivers, priests, and warriors as they did. Michael Tommasi as a philosopher was something of a blend of all these types.

Tommasi's narrator in *Thinking Life* is a different sort of man. Troubled, out of place, out of time, successful but dissatisfied. Doubtless he will strike some readers as irascible, perhaps at times as bitter, and this may put some people off. I understand. Yet I am also sympathetic to the perspective from which Tommasi wrote. The future of which his work in part is a gloomy oracle, the future he most dreaded, has come to pass. Our connection to the natural world has been utterly dissolved. Nature-preserves flourish across our continent, no doubt; but since to visit them we must travel, park, and pay, I'm not sure we can enjoy them. We certainly can't experience ourselves as really at home in nature, dwelling in it, at one with it. So permeated is our world today by technology and distracting devices—it's far more artificial than Tommasi could ever have imagined. Even the necessities of a human life, and our deepest thoughts and innermost feelings, have been twisted into marketable commodities, subject to manipulation by the shamans of fashion and faddishness.

And what of education, the traditional source of resistance to the dominance of the popular and the practical, of ignorance and deceit? Education has become just another mode of business. In the contemporary university the serious study of ideas, books, and beauty, the study of the liberal arts—which is to say the *liberating*, the *freeing* disciplines—ranks among the lowest of priorities, inferior even to economic- and social-engineering schemes. Education is considered at best a meretricious ornament, at worst an impediment to job-training.

And how sadly prescient were Tommasi's ruminations on the future of philosophy! These days philosophy is virtually non-existent, philosophy as the love of wisdom, as joy in intellectual creativity, as radical exploration and the exuberant subversion of entrenched pieties. Philosophy as free-spiritedness. Today there is only the "philosophy profession," in which there is very much profession and very little philosophy.

But I exaggerate. I am not one of those who scoff at contemporary philosophy as stale or as hopelessly obscure (though far too much of it is just that). I appreciate philosophical analysis and rigorous, even pedantic, scholarship. I don't aspire to produce such work myself, but I am grateful to those who do. The problem from my point of view has less to do with the work the professionals produce than with their stifling of work composed in a different style for different ends. Ask yourself: Would a respectable university press publish Plato's *Phaedo* today? And as for Nietzsche— your average acquisitions editor wouldn't read past the first page of any one of his prefaces. Certainly they would never publish Tommasi's little book. It doesn't fit neatly into their established categories. The work moreover is a relentless critique of all they are and do.

But if Tommasi's book were only critical, a rejection of modern culture and academic philosophy, and nothing besides, it would be much less stimulating than it is. His narrator too. Thankfully there is more to the man than his occasional fits of fury. His rage fuels an affirmative drive to health and well-being. And his struggle to incorporate art into his philosophy, and philosophy into his life, adds a fruitful substance to his story.

Richard Rorty was an eloquent proponent of the idea that philosophy is a form of art. Philosophy as poetry. It's a pity he knew nothing of his great predecessor, for Michael Tommasi strove not only to conceive of philosophy as art, but actually to practice philosophy artistically himself. In substance as well as style his aim was a creative intellectuality, and his interweaving of philosophy and fiction in this particular book is a testament to his craft, or at least to his aspiration thereto.

Therefore in the spirit of Tommasi's work, I conclude my own contribution to this little volume with two stories, each in its way confirming my admiration of Tommasi's conception of the life of creative philosophical freedom, and my desire—my innate disposition, really—to follow his example.

Umberto Eco encountered Tommasi's work as a young man, and the impact on his life and thought was profound, as he reported himself in at least one early essay (I discuss this in *The Thinker-Artist*). Eco's summer home in Monte Cerignone is but five miles from my wife's hometown of Mercatino Conca. And since the small, medieval Monte Cerignone has no space for a grocery store, Eco used to do his shopping in Mercatino, just down the street from my in-laws' house. I myself never met the man, but my wife and her mother encountered him often, and both were friendly with his resident housekeeper. On one occasion Professor Eco was kind enough to talk at length with Francesca over an espresso in a bar across the street from the *supermercato*. During the conversation, while speaking of my interest in Plato and Nietzsche as philosopher-artists, and my unwillingness to conform to the contemporary model of professionalized philosopher, Francesca mentioned my studies of Michael Tommasi. Eco's eyes immediately lit up, she later told me, and he threw back his head and smiled. A great man, he exclaimed, and a powerful influence. Tommasi's conception of the philosopher as a "thinker-artist" (Eco employed the English expression) was transformative, he said, lost for a moment apparently in memories of his youth—though he did insist, as an aside, that the expression is aesthetically objectionable, the "-er" in "thinker" and the "ar-" in "artist" an unpleasant juxtaposition in the mouth. "But as to the substance of the matter, and more to the point," he continued, "I much prefer an experimental philosophy infused with creativity and beauty to a petty evidentialism, to objectivity at all costs and the stultifying banalities of the ever-popular naive realism. And as to what precisely we should label such activity," he added, "ask your husband what Plato and Nietzsche would count as philosophy, and let's dismiss with a wave of the hand the cavils of those who are professors and nothing more."

But to speak of those professors who are something more than academics, those few who aspire to live philosophy: a colleague in my department recently had occasion to visit the university health center. While tending to his sprained wrist the nurse on duty asked whether he was a professor and, if so, of what discipline. To his reply that, "Yes, I teach philosophy," she remarked, "Ah, mm-hmm, I figured." And what did she mean by that, he asked. "Well, I don't know," she said, choosing her words thoughtfully. "It's just that you seem so... so *free*."

Freedom is not the spiritual condition of your typical professor of philosophy. Never has been. But it ought to be. Today and always.